TODD S[illegible] PRESENTS:

THE VAMPIRE CONNOISSEUR

Nightmare Press
Louisville, KY

But like all of us, Vinson delivered the dead bodies he created to our parasites, the imps; bodies for disposal which would otherwise rot in plain sight of Mankind, be pondered and investigated. Exposed corpses were too dangerous for us, a tiny minority stalking the world of fragile mortals. Buried bodies were discovered too often. And new technology? iPhones with cameras, still shots or videos uploaded for eternity on the internet highway revealed us to the billions of spiteful people on the planet, the villagers with pitchforks.

-Parasites: A Tale of Route 66

Edited by Todd Sullivan
Cover by Luke Spooner

Thank you for reading! If you like the book, please leave a review on Amazon and Goodreads. Reviews help authors and publishers spread the word.

To keep up with more Nightmare Press news, join the Anubis Press Dynasty on Facebook.

TABLE OF CONTENTS

1. THE RED ANGEL
by Lisa Hario

2. A VISIT FROM SAINT VIC
By Gordon Linzner

3. GIVE ME MY SIN AGAIN
By Tony Pisculli

4. THE SOLUTION
By Michael S. Collins

5. WHAT LITTLE REMAINS
By Paul Alex Gray

6. A FIEND INDEED
By Nicholas Stella

7. THE SUN SETS NONETHELESS
By Priscilla Bettis

8. FINCH
By James Pyne

9. A COLD DISH
By Lonnie Bricker

10. POEM OF THE RIVERBANK
By Gary Robbe

11. DISSIDENT
Idea by Jade Kupkin
Written by Max Carrey

12. SPLINTERS
By Keawe Melina Patrick

13. INVADERS IN WALLACHIA
By Luke Frostick

14. CHILDREN OF LAMIA
By Jacob Floyd

15. PARASITES: A TALE OF ROUTE 66
By B.J. Thrower

16. TAKE ME HOME TONIGHT
By Troy Diffenderfer

THE RED ANGEL

by

Lisa Hario

I saw the Red Angel the night Thomas died.

After the lamps were blown out, only a few shafts of moonlight reached in through the shutters. It was enough to see the small shapes on the twenty cots in the ward. When the sisters made their rounds, their shoes clopped on the wood floor, so we pulled up our blankets to pretend to sleep.

I listened to Thomas in the bed next to me. His breath whistled like wind through a crack. The sound grew quieter, and I counted as the time between each wheeze grew longer. Finally, after counting to sixty, I knew his breath had stopped.

Thomas had made it longer than most, to the age of ten. I heard a voice whispering the Latin that was so familiar. This voice was soothing and sweet, but I didn't recognize it as one of the sisters.

I raised myself up on my elbows. A small shadow leaned over Thomas, holding his hand. I moved to get a better look, and the mattress squeaked.

The shadow turned without a sound. I saw her in the moonlight, a little girl with eyes that glowed like a cat.

She put a finger to her lips and smiled as if we were sharing a secret.

Quick and silent as a hawk, she was gone.

Thomas had told me the story of the Red Angel.

We were in the courtyard on a warm spring day, less than a week after I arrived. I was still walking, but I could no longer run. I had walked the trails under the eyes of the sisters until short of breath, then sat on a bench next to Thomas.

The fountain was the angel Michael spearing Satan. I wondered if he could spear our sickness, because it should be easy after the Devil. The other angel statues scattered on the garden trails looked serene and kindly. Did both angels promise to heal us?

"None of them look like the Red Angel. She's the one who visits us," Thomas said as he stretched.

"You've seen an angel?" I said.

"Once." Thomas shrugged. "She only comes at night, and chooses one of us."

"Chooses for what?"

"To bring to God," he said. "She takes the ones just hanging on, when the doctor can't help them feel better. She carries them up to heaven."

"Why doesn't she take all of us?" I said. That seemed far easier than choosing one by one.

"I don't know. She's the soul of a girl who died. The angel was so sad to leave her friends behind she stayed to guide the rest of us."

"What does she look like?"

"Red," he said. "Her hair is bright red, the color of blood."

The next night I awoke to see the Red Angel sitting next to me.

She sat in the chair by my bed like any other visitor. A ray of moonlight showed me a girl, maybe a little younger than me, with a heart shaped face and curly red hair. Her hands were serenely folded in her lap and she sat perfectly still. She wore a plain black dress but didn't shiver from the cold.

I opened my mouth to tell her I wasn't ready. I hadn't said my prayers today. In mass I had dreamed of her. The sweats had not come this night, and I had eaten well that day. I did not want to meet God yet.

She put a finger to her lips, then took my hand. She was warm to the touch, her skin a healthy pink.

"I know you're not ready." She squeezed my hand. "I'm not here for that."

"What are you here for?"

"You heard me. Not many can hear me."

"Of course I heard you, you were so loud," I said.

Her mouth twitched, and I couldn't understand why.

"Are you the Red Angel?" I said.

She smiled, but it was sad. "They call me that. My name is Claire."

"Anne," I said. I saw no reason not to give her my name. "Are you a ghost? Thomas said you died here."

She shook her head. “No, I was never here when I was sick.” She looked around the ward, cat eyes drinking in the small bodies on the little cots.

“Then what are you?”

“Different.” Her eyes bore into mine. “I won't lie, but I won't answer all your questions.” She studied me from head to toe, and for a moment I saw flames flicker in her cat eyes. “You have a little longer. Before you die.”

It was the first time the words had been said. Even my sister shied from saying death. I should have been shocked but I was relieved. Finally, someone knew and would tell me plain.

“If you're not an angel, how do you know?” I said. The doctor had examined me many times before I was taken to the ward.

“I can smell your sickness.” She pointed to my belly. “It is there now, but it spreads through the rest of your body. When your blood can no longer carry life you will die.”

That was it then. The Angel not only knew I was dying, she knew how.

“How long?” I asked. My voice was strangely calm.

“I don't know. Probably a few months. You won't make your next birthday.”

“I’m just a child, I’m too young to die.” I knew it was a lie, even as I said it. A brother of mine had not lived to his first year.

She raised an eyebrow. “Children die before they are born. Death doesn’t care.”

Did I want that to be true, or a lie? I wasn't sure which was worse.

“Why did you give last rites to Thomas?” I said.

"Perhaps it helps his soul rest." She shrugged. "He believed that. It brought comfort to us both. Sometimes that is all a rite is meant to do."

"You talk like prayer is just words."

"It is. Because words are always powerful, commended to God or not."

"Do you believe in anything?"

"Mercy." I felt soft lips on my forehead, and she was gone.

The next morning, I was told Elizabeth had died.

We all knew what the ward was, even if the sisters refused to speak of it.

This was the place children came to die.

Adults never told us. When we asked how sick we were or what all the tests meant the doctors told us to rest up and we would get better. The sisters were kind, and told us to make confession and pray. They talked about how to get to heaven, but when we asked if we were going there soon the sisters told us not to worry. By the time one of us came to the ward, we knew. Each of us found out in our own way.

Last winter was harsh. I got sick, just like my sister. But Charlotte grew rosy cheeked while the chill never left me. Eating a full meal grew harder, and at night I ached and sweat. On the first day of spring I thought the warm sun would chase my illness away. My sisters and I raced in the park.

I do not remember falling, but I remember waking up. The doctor had been sent for, and he listened to my chest as he had done many times that winter. His wizened eyes tried to stay calm over his pursed lips. He left the room to confer with my parents. They thought they were far enough away I couldn't hear, but one word was enough.

Consumption. It had taken my aunt, and it would take me, too.

Claire didn't come every night. She visited for a week straight, then Claire was gone with no word as to when she would return. When the moon was high in the sky, I counted the nights until I saw her again. I reached eight once and wondered if she had left for good.

The next night, Claire returned.

Most nights, Claire slipped in bed beside me, her cool hand in mine as we talked. I tried to stay awake as long as I could, even as we spoke until the moon faded in the sky, until Claire kissed me goodbye for the night. Sometimes the sweats would be upon me, and she held me without words until it was time for her to go. No one heard us in the ward. She ducked low when the sisters walked by.

I was filled with curiosity about Claire and her world. She rarely answered with more than the barest of facts if I asked where she lived. She never told me why she was in the city. The pieces of her past I learned were tantalizing treats, but never enough to satisfy my desire to know all about her.

“Were you like me once?” I asked one night, once again trying to pull a little more from her.

“Yes,” she said, this time being more open than usual. “But it was a long time ago and I don't remember much of it.”

“How did you become what you are?” I said.

"I died," Claire said, "with a power greater than life or death in my blood. That brought me back."

"Why are you still a child?" I said.

"I am not a child, I just look like one," she said.

"Do adults think you don't understand anything?"

"Yes. That's why I rarely speak with them."

"Why do you come to me?"

"Maybe I'm bored. The adults believe you can't take the knowledge of your coming death, and so they lie to all of you. But that means children like you don't receive the comfort you need."

I knew it was true. Why couldn't anyone just be honest? Why did I have to sneak to find out the truth of my illness? Talking with Claire made me feel better for the coming day, and gave me something to look forward to in the night.

"Why aren't you scared?" I said.

"Death continues my life like every other hunter. Why would I be frightened of something I know so well? The people who keep you here are the cowards."

"You've seen a lot of death. You've caused some of it." It was a statement, not a question. I waited for a denial, but there was none.

Family could only come on certain days and certain times. Sundays were visiting days, and my parents came in the afternoon, following mass. We shared a picnic on the lawn.

I wanted to tell them about Claire. I burst with the need to say I had a new friend. But Claire was precious to me. She was the one thing that was mine and only mine. Claire insisted she wasn't an angel, but she was my angel, and I would not risk anyone taking that from me.

My parents talked like everything was normal. Mom asked me what medicines the doctors gave me and told me to be a good girl. Dad asked if I needed any more books. I missed my sisters, and asked how they were.

Even if I didn't know, their faces when they visited would have told me. I saw it in the way Mom almost cried when she hugged me goodbye, her hands shaking. Dad choked up, but managed to take a breath from his cigar.

They always insisted that I would return home when I got better. I thought so too at first. My first weeks I prayed in the chapel every day. I told God if He healed me I would stop teasing the little ones, or study harder, or do my best to be good. I confessed every sin I thought I had committed in my life.

But I still grew weaker, the pain more intense no matter how much I prayed.

One night Claire took me up to the roof. I was able to walk most of the way, but we had to stop a few times on the stairs for me to catch my breath. Claire said nothing, simply offered her arm for when I wanted to take it.

I peered over the edge of the wall down to the street, and for a moment wondered if this was a better way to leave the ward. The moment passed when I gazed up to see the beautiful stars. In the streets below I searched for my home, and felt a stab of loneliness for my sisters.

"Do you have a family?" I said. "I miss mine terribly."

I was hesitant at first, but once I started the words tumbled out of me. Of my sisters, Charlotte and Lucy. Of our little brick house and the room I shared with them.

"I am never going back there, am I?" I whispered. "I am never going home again."

I should have sobbed, but I only blinked away a few tears. Claire's cool hand pressed into mine, and I was grateful for the wordless comfort.

"Where is home for you?" I asked.

She shrugged. "I rarely get to stay in one place very long."

"Will you be leaving soon?"

"No." Her hand squeezed tight. She looked over the edge, her eyes intent on the street below.

"You must have had parents," I said. "What happened to them?"

"I killed them." She spoke with no hint of joy or regret. She turned to look me in the eye, her face expressionless.

"You murdered your parents." I gripped the wall, and the rough stone scratched my fingers.

"Murder is something humans do to each other. The word doesn't apply to me."

"Why did you kill them?"

"Mother was an accident." For a moment, her eyes flashed with regret. "I didn't know how to control myself. With Father, it was him or me. I chose him."

I walked away, hugging myself.

"Are you afraid of me, Anne?" Now her voice tinged with-- what? Tears?

"Why wouldn't I be?" I said, turning back to her. "You're a killer."

She reached out and touched my hand. "Do you think I would ever hurt you?"

I met her eyes. They held naked pleading as she gripped my hand. Claire's eyes, kissed by fire that glowed in the dark. My Claire, who came to me and comforted me during my illness.

I squeezed her hand. "No. You wouldn't."

Wednesday afternoon we had an hour of art time. I drew an angel with curly red hair wearing a black dress. I made her eyes green to glow like a cat.

I did not see Sister Margaret. She cleared her throat and yanked the drawing from the table. Beady eyes looked down at me from her starched habit.

"What are you drawing?" she said, her hand crumpling the paper.

"An angel." No need to say which angel I was drawing. I stood up straight. After all, they couldn't stop Claire from seeing me if Claire wished.

"An angel in red?" She spat the color *red* as if somehow it was the spawn of Satan.

"There can be a red angel."

Sister Margaret brought me to the Mother Superior, and ranted about how I was spreading tales. This Red Angel was just a fancy of bored children confined to their beds, God bless them. But no one should get them worked up over a story.

The Mother Superior said nothing through the tirade. I had only met the older woman a few times, and inwardly trembled in fear. Finally, when Sister Margaret stopped for a breath, Mother said in her British accent, "I will speak with her privately."

As soon as Sister Margaret left, she said "You have seen her, then? The Red Angel?"

I looked down at my hands.

"I am not angry with you, Anne. I couldn't harm Claire even if I wished to."

"How do you know her name?" I blurted out.

I looked up, certain to see suspicion or rage, but I only saw curiosity.

"She must be fond of you," the Mother Superior said. "Claire rarely visits."

I bit my lip. The Mother Superior set a tray of scones in front of me. I took a small bite, not sure if this was a trick.

"Do you know her?" I said.

A smile. "Yes, a long time ago. When I was younger than you."

The Mother Superior had a full head of white hair, and a wrinkled face. She was as old as my grandmother. I refused to think of how old that made Claire.

"Claire and I were at the same orphanage, back in Europe. She was young in truth. Back then she went among the sick so much everyone thought she would become a nun. I don't know if she hid what she was very well, or if people simply didn't want to see. She didn't stay long after I came."

"What happened? Was she adopted?"

"A man came and took her away." She looked off into the distance, lost for a moment in days long ago. "I don't know what happened to her between that day and the night I saw her again. One night, while working late I saw Claire. Make no mistake, I only saw her because she let me. She promised to only take the dying. She's as good as her word, Claire."

"Why do you let her come here?" I said. "Aren't you supposed to save us?"

"I doubt there is anything I could do to stop her if I wanted to," the Mother Superior said, taking a bite of a scone. "Claire's hand is gentler than God's. I do not think Lord Jesus meant for children to die, but what God wants and what God does are different things." She made a dismissive gesture. "You will not speak of this, or her. Now go off and pretend I gave you a proper scolding."

I was alone in the chapel with my prayers when Claire visited. I knew she was there before I turned around.

"I thought you couldn't come in the daytime. Or in here." I gestured to the statue of Jesus.

"I can. Most of the time it is too dangerous." She sat down in the pew next to me.

"Have you seen God, Claire?"

"No. I don't particularly care if I do."

"Have you seen the devil?"

"I saw a devil, but I don't think he was *the* devil. He made me what I am."

"Was he the man who took you away from the orphanage?"

"Yes."

"Did he make you what you are?" I asked.

She shook her head. "No. My blood has a power he wished to use for his own ends. He was not kind to me."

Claire, who braved discovery to see me, who was unflinching in the face of my pain, now had her jaw set.

"What did he do to you?" I whispered. A small fist curled in my belly. What would make my Claire so upset?

She blinked, shaking herself as if waking from a dream. "Never you mind, Anne. It was a long time ago."

Curiosity still burned in me, but I knew the look on her face. I reached out and took her hand. She squeezed, and I never felt more at peace than I did in that moment. "You can smell it, can't you?"

"Yes," Claire said. "The sickness will win soon."

"Is that why you're here?"

"I wanted to see you in sunlight."

My heart was in my throat. I wanted so much for Claire to be with me. Her visits brought me peace. "Please stay," was all I could say.

"I can't. But I will be with you at the end, I promise."

I had resolved to ask her as I lay awake at night waiting for her, but now the moment was here, terror paralyzed me. If I waited until she came again it might be too late. I knew I wanted to be with Claire. I didn't know if it meant giving up Heaven for more time on earth.

I turned to her. "Can you make me like you?"

She looked me straight in the eye. "No."

"But if you don't, I'll die."

"Humans are supposed to die. Becoming like me isn't supposed to happen. My parents thought they were saving my life when they gave me the blood. They thought they could keep me from changing. They were wrong."

I tore my hand from hers and stood as straight as I could. "You would *prefer* to be dead? You prefer *me* to be dead than with you?"

"I don't know if I would have wanted this or not. I don't remember when I was like you. I can't tell you what is better because I don't know any other existence."

"You're going to let me die." Saying those words felt like being torn in two.

"You're not strong enough for my world. At least this way you will die still being you."

"Then why do you bother befriending me? Why do you dangle hope in front of me if you're just going to refuse me?"

"What do you hope for? A better life? I can't give you that."

"God, Claire. I want to grow up." I slammed my hand down on the pew.

"You can't and neither can I," Claire said. She stood rigid, her hands balled into fists. "We're both trapped by what we can't control. Getting angry at me doesn't change it. I didn't make you sick and I can't cure you of it."

"I want to run again. I'm scared, Claire." I turned away, blinking back tears. "I don't know what happens after."

"Of course you're scared." Her voice sounded gentler than I had ever heard it. She reached out to touch the tear on my cheek. "No one knows what

happens after. I only know I can't hear someone after death. It takes a different power than mine."

"Does death hurt?" I said.

"By the end you can't feel pain."

"I don't want to die." My voice sounded feeble and wobbly.

"I know." She laid a hand on my forehead. "It will happen, regardless of what you want."

"It isn't fair!"

For once, I cried. I had prayed to be healed, waiting for an answer from God. While the pain always returned, the answer from God never came. Now the thought crept into my head: was God a lie, the same way the doctors lied when they said we would get better? But if God was a lie, it was one everyone believed.

"It isn't," Claire said, and wiped away my tears.

She held me as I cried for the one and only time for what could have been.

"You will not make your next birthday."

As the days grew colder, I knew she was right. I could only walk for a bit before I was short of breath, and was wheeled by the sisters. No matter what I had done, no matter how good or obedient I was, I became sicker. No bargain I asked God for was agreed to. If God was a lie, I only had Claire to turn to for help. But Claire would not save me.

The trees had been full of leaves when I came. Now they were turning colors and starting to fall. I watched the flowers wilt in the garden. I saw the remains of a rabbit after the fox had eaten it. Animals are born, and we all find joy in it. But animals also die, just maybe not as loud as they were born.

We all die in the end. I had been given no choice. What sin had I committed that was so great to allow me to suffer? But if my illness was bad luck, I could not pray for luck to change. If God could make me well but chose not to, I had no one to ask to be well.

Maybe Claire was right, or maybe the world had more compassion than she said. But either way, Claire had been the only one I could speak to. My friends were gone. All except Claire.

Once when Claire visited, we had talked about our mothers. “What songs did your mother sing to you, when she wanted you to sleep?” Claire had asked.

I hummed a few lullabies.

“It must be a sweet memory, of your mother singing to you.”

I had smiled. “I have many good memories of my mother.”

“I only remember my mother's photograph.”

Cold took me. I could no longer stay warm. At night as I sweat my bones ached. Even short walks were beyond me. On my skin, blue veins crossed through purple bruises. I stopped feeling hungry, and the scent of food only made my stomach curl.

Mom and Dad came to read out loud to me. I heard the sisters whisper about getting the priest.

The doctors gave me medicine in the morning. As evening grew closer, I skipped my next dose.

The long day wore to night and I began to doubt. I had been angry last time we spoke, when I broke into tears. Would Claire still come? But she had made a promise, and I clung to that.

I needn't have feared. Claire came when the moon rose high.

I reached my hand out, and Claire took me in a hug. She lay her forehead on mine and closed her eyes. I gripped her tightly as I could, even though my hold was weak.

She stood, stroking my hair and face. The tears were still wet. Despite all my blankets, I was cold.

"Will it hurt?" I croaked out.

"No." She squeezed my hand. "You will hurt far less than you do now."

That, I knew, was all she could promise. "I love you, Claire."

"I love you too, Anne." For the first time, I heard her voice crack. "I bring my final gift. Are you ready?"

I had been struggling to breathe the last few days. I watched the healthy children in the garden through the window during the day. I knew I would never join them again.

"Yes."

She stroked my hand, then turned over my palm. Her thumb traced the pulse on my wrist. She opened her mouth, just slightly, to reveal sharp little fangs. She met my eyes. I nodded.

Claire raised my wrist to her lips. She was right. It didn't hurt.

A VISIT FROM SAINT VIC

by
Gordon Linzner

Vladimir Vicuna eyed the scrawny youth from head to foot. His frown deepened.

The lad's fingers twitched. He poked at his gums, reaching under the upper lip. A bright red elf suit, more crimson than fresh blood, hung limply from his shoulders, its white trim already dingy.

What idiot considered this wretch a good candidate for turning? Vicuna could only assume it was accidental, one of their kind either in a hurry or excessively hungry, rather than an intentional transformation.

Vicuna shrugged. He'd mentored worse. None of whom had yet gone on to make him proud, but even the undead needed to hope.

"I assume this is your first time, son?" His voice lowered to a soft whisper. The suburban street was nearly deserted, but that was no guarantee some soul would not be up and about, poking around in their home, perhaps anxiously peering out the window from time to time. The living, especially children, often had difficulty falling asleep on Christmas Eve.

Which was, in fact, the very thing his kind counted on.

"First time for what?" the boy whispered back.

"The hunt." Vicuna adjusted his false beard. He ran a bony hand along his own crimson outfit, checking that the padding remained securely fastened to his abdomen. A cold, bitter wind blew between rows of single-family houses. Naturally – unnaturally might be more accurate – the wintry blast had no effect on Vicuna and his charge, save to ruffle a few hairs.

The lad straightened, slightly defiant. That was not a promising sign. "Not my first. Not exactly. I've had a taste."

"In the pens, I'd guess. This is the real thing. Your name, again?"

"Eric. Eric Rob..."

"Eric will do. Well, Eric, you could not pick a better night for easing your way into this lifestyle – if you'll excuse the lack of a more appropriate word." Vicuna smirked. He never tired of that joke.

"How so?"

"Normally, one needs substantial finesse to gain the trust of your prey. Developing that skill takes time and patience. However, on Christmas Eve, as you should still be new enough to remember, the living are usually a little more accepting. They actually expect a stranger to come calling."

"Here's what I don't understand," Eric countered. "We are stronger than them. Faster. Less vulnerable. Why do we go to the bother of invading their homes, given all the restrictions?

Why don't we just take out whatever strays we find in alleyways or tunnels or public parks?"

"That's fine, if you wish to draw unwanted attention to bodies piling up. Also, as you will discover in time, such easy prey tends to be less satisfying." With a conciliatory smile, Vicuna patted the youth's shoulder. "I understand your eagerness. I, too, was impetuous when I first turned. Of course, it was much easier to get away with that kind of carelessness a century ago."

Eric scowled.

"You must also learn to better conceal your emotions, Eric. Our kind have too many tells as it is." Vicuna tugged at the burlap bag flung over his shoulder, shifting its hollow contents. "Notice the light shining in that upper room of this house. Do not speak. Only observe. You will have your opportunity soon enough."

Vicuna leapt silently onto the eave above the porch to face the second floor bedroom window. With a shrug, Eric followed.

A young girl, six or seven years old, peeked out at them. Her eyes widened.

Vicuna gestured for her to open the window.

"It's you!" she exclaimed, raising the pane. "You're..."

Vicuna pressed a finger to his lips for silence. "We do not wish to wake anyone else. May we enter?"

"Who is that?" She pointed past Vicuna.

"My helper, Erich." Vicuna stressed the Germanic pronunciation with a moist hiss. "Could you kindly invite us in? We ask that you do so freely, of your own will."

"Of course. Please come in." She opened the window wider, then stepped aside.

"Thank you."

Vicuna slid through the gap with a single, well-practiced motion. Eric followed, less elegantly, his left foot catching briefly on the sill. Vicuna strode past the child, toward her bedroom door, as if heading for the decorated tree that would inevitably dominate the living room. "Be a good girl and promise not to follow us. We don't want to spoil the surprises. We will let ourselves out."

Eric gave him a querulous look. Vicuna shook his head, mouthed 'too young.'

As the child's bedroom door closed behind them, Vicuna moved to the parents' room. A moment's appraisal confirmed both adults slept soundly. The father looked more promising. Vicuna bent over him, exhaled a numbing mist onto the exposed neck, and delicately sank needle sharp fangs into the jugular. He fed for less than a minute before pulling away, leaving barely a mark. With a wave of his hand, he signaled Eric they were to leave.

The youth opened his mouth, closed it, and obeyed, sulking.

Once outside, Eric challenged Vicuna.

"Why did you barely take a taste? Why didn't you allow me to feed on the woman? I understand sparing the child, but I'm ravenous!"

"Baby steps, Eric. Or, rather, baby nibbles. I sense the depth of your hunger. That is precisely why you must learn to exercise control. We do not want fatalities, nor do we wish to turn anyone."

Anyone else, he added silently. "Keeping a low profile is not easy."

"I still don't see..."

"You'll become aware of another benefit as your palate develops. Sampling different flavors is far more satisfying than gorging on a one-note meal. I like to picture Christmas Eve as a buffet night."

Eric grimaced.

Vicuna sighed. "You'll see. At the next house, you will take the lead, now you've seen how it's done." With that, he unfastened his false beard and handed it to his reluctant protege.

The padding would not stay in place against Eric's gaunt frame. Vicuna finally shoved it into the burlap sack, adding to the rags and empty boxes that gave the illusion of bulk.

This time their inviter was a four-year-old boy. In his anxiousness to seek permission, Eric spoke curtly. Vicuna had to add the 'freely, of your own will' line to cover their bases. He also was later forced to pull his feasting apprentice from the mother, leaving an awkward wound on her neck and almost waking her.

Otherwise, the process went quite smoothly, for a first time.

As the night progressed, Vicuna allowed Eric more leeway, taking turns with him at the feeding, finally letting the young one enter an adults' bedroom alone while he remained in the hall, listening should his intervention be required.

"This is our last house for tonight," Vicuna advised the youth. "It's getting late. Or, rather, early. Near dawn, anyway."

The two stood at the far edge of the suburban community. Their final house stood apart from the others, more ornate, yet slightly shabby.

Vicuna leapt to the second floor eave.

"Can I at least have more time with this one?" Eric complained, patting his stomach.

Vicuna shook his head. "One's appetite should always retain an edge. It keeps one alert. Another lesson you'll come to appreciate in time."

Eric leaned toward the bedroom window. The curtain was closed but translucent. Against the yellow glow of the room's nightlight, he spotted the silhouette of a small figure moving about.

He rapped his knuckles on the windowpane. The figure stopped moving, presumably in response.

"Do you know me?" Eric called through the glass. He indicated his red felt suit.

No reply.

"You must."

Still no response.

Condescendingly, Eric added, "Little child, little child, let me come in."

"Not by the hair on your chinny-chin-chin." An uncomfortable hollowness infused the high-pitched, sing-song reply.

Vicuna tapped Eric's elbow. "Something is wrong here. We're done for the night."

"But I'm still hungry!"

"You will always be hungry. It is our nature."

"I say we do it!"

Vicuna shook his head. He was much too familiar with this attitude among the newly turned.

"How exactly do you hope to accomplish your plan, Eric? You know the rule. It's one of our first lessons: our kind cannot enter where we are not invited."

"Stupid rule."

"I didn't create it, any more than I created the sun that burns our flesh, or our lack of a mirror reflection. It is what it is."

Eric turned away from Vicuna to rap on the window again, harder.

"Let me in!"

"Or what? You'll huff and puff and blow the house down?" The sing-song tenor pitched even higher.

"Eric," Vicuna hissed. "That's enough. Dawn is less than an hour away. We need time to reach our lair!"

The youth glared at him. "You will not infect me with your fears, old one!"

"There is a difference between fear and discretion."

"Not that I see!" Eric turned his back on Vicuna to once more pound on the glass. "Let me in! Don't you want your presents?"

"Have you turnips?" asked the voice.

"What? No! I mean, yes! Of course! All you can eat, and more!"

"I don't believe you. I say we wait until morning, and go to market together, you and I, to purchase some nice, fresh turnips. Yum."

Vicuna leapt from the eave to the ground. “Come away, Eric. Now.”

“No!”

“And lower your voice.”

“I’ll not let some silly child intimidate me! I’ll drain him dry!”

“That is also...” Vicuna shrugged. “You’re on your own, then.” He turned away from the neglected façade of the house and slowly started down the empty street.

Howling in frustration, Eric grabbed the burlap sack they’d dragged up with them and hurled it against the intransigent window.

To both his shock and delight, the glass shattered. Eric leaned forward. He still could not enter, not without an explicit invitation, but if he pulled the curtain aside, got a good view of the teasing brat within, he almost certainly could evoke one.

A pair of tiny hands reached out, grasping his elfin collar. A second pair joined them, tugging hard at his cardboard belt. A third pair followed. A fourth.

He lost count.

Shards of broken glass slashed the bright red suit, digging into the flesh underneath. Eric felt himself dragged through the window frame and onto the hardwood floor within.

He rolled onto his back and looked around. The room was devoid of furnishings; indeed, empty of anything save a score of elf-like creatures, grinning at him under thick snouts, their tiny eyes a-glitter.

Eric glanced behind him.

The window was gone.

Vladimir Vicuna stood before the skeletal figure of Marcello, eldest of their kind in the territory, nine feet tall, reddish eyes sunk deep below thick white brows. No one knew Marcello's last name, or if he even had one. No one who was still around.

"So, Vlad. Eric?" Marcello's reedy voice was nonetheless penetrating.

"I've dealt with worse fledglings." Not much worse, Vicuna added silently, and none of those had returned from their first hunt, either. Still...

"Survive?"

"If he keeps his wits about him. I'd not bet on it. He's headstrong."

Marcello made the rasping sound that, for him, passed for a chuckle. "You," he said, pointing at Vicuna.

"Much like me, yes." Vicuna grinned ruefully. "Yet I somehow made it through the process. Which obviously is why you continue asking me to mentor the new ones."

"Ask?"

Vicuna lowered his eyes. "Order, I mean. I was being polite. There's still no chance of another taking over this duty...?"

"Sleep." Marcello began drifting down the catacomb corridor toward his personal bier.

I didn't think so, Vicuna conceded. His shoulders slumped. Maybe, if Eric actually did somehow survive his final test, these mentoring duties could be shunted over to him in a decade or three.

Who was he kidding? The kid was toast.

Now Vicuna himself needed sleep. Rest up for the coming evening.

Christmas night could also be full of surprises.

GIVE ME MY SIN AGAIN
by
Tony Pisculli

In the coffee shop of last resort—that place on Kuhio that survives by virtue of staying open later than the bars and clubs, collecting the dregs of the evening—Mariano sits alone in a booth big enough for six, waiting for someone to save his life.

He comes here when he can't sleep. Between the cancer and the chemo, that's most nights. He can still manage the walk from his studio on Ala Wai, but not for much longer. He's left with a lot of time to think, and his thoughts are mostly of regret, though lately regret has been displaced by fear.

He digs his thumb into the hard knot of traitorous flesh in his belly. Sometimes he imagines he can feel it move, like an egg sac about to burst.

She'll come, he thinks. *Tonight she'll come. She has to.*

He takes another sip of coffee and winces at the taste. Decaf. But it warms him up. The temperature outside is a tropical 70 degrees, even at this hour, but inside, the air-con is running full tilt, and his blood is thin.

He rattles his cup in the saucer as he sets it down, and the waitress takes that as her cue to swing by with the pot. He covers the cup with his hand and catches her eye to ensure she's not going to pour hot coffee on him. She's done it before. Or if not this one, another one. They all look the same to him now, dressed like men in jeans and t-shirts with name tags in type too small to read. She drops his check on the table and moves on.

When he looks back, Lia is there, having arrived without a sound, as she does. She looks 17, but he knows she's older than that. She has a fake ID in her wallet that says she's 22, but he knows she's older than that, too.

"Don't come to the club anymore, Mariano," she says without preamble. She unzips her heavy leather riding jacket but leaves her sunglasses on.

"I needed to see you. I have something for you."

"I heard. Next time leave it with the doorman."

"There won't be a next time," he says.

"Fine. What do you have?" she says again, her eyes invisible behind dark lenses.

For a moment he thinks he's engaged her sympathy, that she's asking about his condition. She knows about the tumor; she doesn't know it's metastasized. He reaches across the table, but she leans back and folds her arms, slouching in the booth, her leather jacket squeaking against the worn red vinyl.

"Show me," she says.

"Just like that?"

"Oh, excuse me. The niceties. How are you, Mariano? How was your day? Did you eat any solid food?"

"Did *you*?" he says with venom. He's here to beg a favor, but he falls so quickly into old patterns. He can't afford that now. "I'm sorry," he says, "can we start over?"

Lia nods, almost imperceptibly.

"I have a new doctor," he says.

"Is he good?"

"He's young. He's fascinated with my blood. Always in need of another sample." He pushes up his coat sleeve to show her his arm. "You see? Like a user of heroin. I don't mind. The punks leave me alone. They think a junkie who has lived so long must be formidable." He rolls his sleeve back down. "And you, Lia? How are you?"

"The same," she says.

"Alone," he ventures. "You don't have to be."

"What do you want, Mariano? Money? I told you before—"

"Maybe I just wanted to see you. Is that so hard to believe?"

"Yes."

"Lia…"

"I believed you once," she says.

"How long are you going to punish me for that?"

"I'm protecting myself," she says. "I'm protecting you."

"I don't want to be protected from you!" He slams his fist on the tabletop, making the silverware jump. Heads turn at the sound of his outburst.

"We've had this conversation before." She zips up her jacket. "The sun'll be up soon."

"No, wait." He reaches into his coat, produces a photograph from the inner pocket. "I was going through some old things. I found this."

He slides the photo across the table. It's an old black and white, nearly square, with a white border. A young couple on the beach, Diamond Head in the background. The boy has dark, wavy hair, olive skin and a smile that says he's unlocked the secrets of the universe. The girl is Lia in a modest one-piece bathing suit and no make-up, but the same jet black hair and intelligent eyes. She wears a small silver cross on a delicate chain.

"Do you remember?" he says. "The summer we met."

"Memories are like milk," she says, pushing the photo back. "They sour with age."

"Keep it," he says. "It's the only thing I have to give you. You'll save my lawyer the trouble."

"Throw it away," she says. "Spare us both."

He blinks. His eyes are wet, and suddenly he's mortified she'll think he's crying, but it's just old man rheum. He dabs at the corners of his eyes with his napkin.

"You're dying," she says, not unkindly. "I can smell it on you." She reaches for him. Her skin is cool but smooth and perfect, unchanged by time; his sallow, wrinkled and spotted with age. It's been so long since anyone touched him with, if not affection, at least sympathy.

"Remember our first kiss?" he says.

"Under the banyan tree."

"Before that. Our *first* kiss." He unfolds his hand from hers and presses it flat against her palm—two saints, sharing a prayer. "Palm to palm …"

"… is holy palmers' kiss. I remember. You wanted to kiss me, and I was too shy. I'd just seen *Romeo and Juliet.*"

"I promised I'd take you to see it again. I never got the chance."

"Star-crossed lovers," she says. "They die in the end."

"But first they love." He twines his fingers with hers, kisses them gently. "Lia, please."

She pulls away. The spell is broken.

"I can't give you what you want," she says. "It's a sin."

"A sin? A sin? What about your club boys? How many now? A hundred? A thousand? You'll go down on all of Christendom but you're still saving your virginity like a precious flower. For what?"

"Is that what you want? What I give them?"

"No," he says, louder than he intended. He drops his voice. "No. I want to be with you."

"What you're asking for is a bond stronger than marriage. It's forever. You couldn't commit to me for a *summer*."

"I've changed," he says.

"Have you? Or are you just afraid to die?"

He slumps back in the booth. He *does* love her, he always has. If the urgency of sex, or survival, momentarily trumped his feelings for her, that doesn't mean they weren't genuine.

"Do you still wear the cross I gave you?" he says.

He sees her stifle the urge to feel for it under her shirt and knows she does.

"Yes," she says.

"Does it still burn?" he says.

"Yes," she whispers.

"Good."

But he doesn't mean it. He feels foolish and old and contemptible. He's spent a lifetime wishing he could go back in time and undo the hurt he did both of them, but he's given up now. He's defeated. At least he's no longer afraid. Fear comes from uncertainty, and now he knows.

"Then this is goodbye," he says. "You won't see me again."

"I hope you find peace."

"Peace," he says. "What I need is forgiveness. Can you offer me that?"

"I can. I have."

"I need to hear you say it."

She looks him in the eye. "I forgive you, Mariano."

"Thank you," he says. He closes his eyes. She's forgiven him before, like she says, forgiven but not forgotten. But this one feels different. Final. He opens his eyes. "Thank you," he says again.

"Let me call you a cab," she says.

"I can manage."

Mariano drops a crumpled five-dollar bill on the table for his coffee and stands. His heart is pounding—maybe it wasn't decaf after all—and he steadies himself against the back of the booth. He feels lightheaded. He should eat when he gets home, but he's not looking forward to another one of those damn smoothies that smell like lawn clippings.

He takes two steps into the parking lot before his knees collapse under him, and he blacks out.

Mariano wakes in an unfamiliar bed and sees Lia sitting beside him.

"Where am I?"

"My apartment."

Her bedroom glows with subtle, recessed lighting and a few well-placed lamps. Heavy blackout curtains guard the windows. Over the dresser hangs a watercolor of a sea turtle by a local painter; Mariano recognizes the style but can't remember the name.

He sees his clothes piled up on a chair in the corner and realizes he's naked beneath the covers.

"What happened?" he says.

"After your grand exit? You collapsed in the parking lot."

"You brought me here? On your motorcycle?"

"I'm stronger than I look."

The image of Lia wrestling his unconscious body onto her bike and roaring through downtown Honolulu with him—where, on the handlebars?—makes him laugh till he coughs. Black humor. It's grotesque, but still, he can't remember the last time he actually laughed out loud.

"That must have been something to see," he says when he can breathe again. "Why here? Why not the hospital?"

"They can't help you now."

He swallows, not sure if she's simply brought him here to make him comfortable in his final moments, or if she's offering something more, the help he asked her for in the diner, the help she refused him.

"I'm surprised you have a bed," he says, "I thought you didn't sleep."

"Camouflage," she says. "For the landlord, maintenance, the occasional delivery." She looks around the room. "And I like this room. It's peaceful. I come in here sometimes to think."

He smooths a wrinkle in the high thread-count top sheet. "But you don't sleep here?"

"You're the first."

He looks at her.

"I don't bring club boys home with me. You're the first man who's ever been in my bed."

"You've been saving it for me."

She opens her mouth as if to object, then smiles. "Perhaps," she says.

"I'm honored."

"You should be."

He detects a hint of promise, but he has to be careful.

"Could I have a glass of water?"

"Of course."

She leaves, and he can hear the cabinet door open, hear her running the tap in the kitchen.

He sits up in bed, arranging the pillows as a backrest. He pulls the covers up to hide his chest, embarrassed by his sagging body. He briefly considers retrieving his shirt from the chair, but he's still light-headed.

When Lia returns, she's naked but for the glass of water she's holding.

He turns his head away.

"Mariano," she says. "Look at me."

He looks.

Her body is framed in the doorway, a pale vision set against the dark of the unlit room beyond. The bedroom lights refract through the water glass, causing a constellation of lights to dance across her flat belly and small, perfect breasts. Her body is hairless save for a dark triangle pointing the way to the holy of holies.

"Is this what you want?" she says, spreading her arms and pivoting slightly on the balls of her feet.

He nods, not trusting himself to speak.

"Are you sure?"

He's never been as certain of anything in his life. He thought he was asking Lia to save his life, but in this instant he knows he'd trade his remaining time on Earth for one night with her.

He knows he shouldn't say anything, not now when he's on the brink of joy, but he has to know. "Why did you change your mind?"

"When you fell..." she starts. She crosses to him, sets the glass down on the nightstand and sits beside him once more. "I thought I would be okay if you walked out that door, if I never saw you again. But when you fell—oh, Mariano, I thought you were dead. And I knew I would never be okay again. Always, in the back of my mind, I thought, someday. But I waited too long. I let you die. *I* betrayed *you*." She's crying now, plump tears sliding down her cheeks. "I've never felt such pain."

He pulls her close, wrapping his arms around her, feels her body shaking with sobs. "Hush now," he says. "It's okay. I didn't die."

"But I thought you did," she says. "I never want to feel that pain again." She lifts her head to look at him, blinking the tears from her eyes. "*Mahal kita*," she says. *I love you.*

"*Ti amo*," Mariano says. "*Voglio stare con te per sempre*."

"Really, Mariano? Forever?"

"Forever," he says.

She leans forward to kiss him. Their lips touch, and suddenly he's seventeen years old again, under a banyan tree with the most beautiful girl in the world, with the trade winds blowing, and the salt water still drying on their skin.

Lia brushes his cheek. "*Mahal ko*," she says. *My love*. She tries to pull the covers down, but he won't let go.

"I'm not young anymore," he says.

"I don't care."

She kisses him again, passionately. Her hand slides under the sheets and up his thigh, dragging her nails, teasing him. He moans with decades of pent up desire. She moves between his legs.

He pushes her away.

"What's wrong?" she says.

He's waited for this moment for nearly sixty years, but now his failing body has betrayed him. "Nothing," he says, close to tears.

"Shh. It's okay," she says. "We can do this the old-fashioned way."

She spins the ring she wears on her index finger, releasing the small, scalpel-like blade.

He covers his crotch. "You're not going to cut me?"

She laughs.

"Not there," she says. "I don't have to hide what I'm doing from you."

"Your club boys don't notice?"

"If they feel anything, they assume it's my teeth," she says.

She takes his hand in hers, pressing their palms together, and smiles. She runs her fingers gently up his arm, feeling the life force pulsing beneath the skin.

In one quick move, she drags her index finger along his wrist, opening up the vein, and quickly presses her lips to the incision.

She drinks.

His cock springs to life, the stiffest it's felt in years, lifting the bed sheets like a toy circus tent. He grabs her free hand, guides it back beneath the sheets and nearly explodes at her touch.

She lets go of his wrist and licks the blood off her lips.

"We'll have time for that later," she says. "All the time in the world."

She makes another incision in her own wrist and offers herself to him.

"Your turn now."

He hesitates, then kisses the wound. He feels her hot blood on his tongue, welling up from the slit in her cool flesh. The flavor is complex, smoky and intoxicating as fine scotch. He drinks greedily, gulping it down.

She has to wean him off.

"Enough," she says. "How do you feel?"

"Hungry," he says with wonder. "I haven't felt hungry in months. Strong. *Alive*."

He sweeps the covers aside and stands up, scooping her up in his arms. She squeals with delight, and he grins. He carries her to the full-length mirror beside her dresser. His erection leads the way like a jaunty compass needle.

His grin fades as he confronts his reflection.

"I'm still old."

"You're only as old as you feel," she says.

"I feel ..." He lowers her feet to the ground, and she stands, her body pressed against his, cradled in his arm. "I feel like I'm growing."

"Growing?"

"Yes."

He flexes his biceps. His muscles are expanding, filling out. He looks stronger, more vital. His wrinkles diminish as the flesh fills out beneath his skin. He rubs his suddenly itchy scalp and laughs to discover new growth there.

Lia untangles herself from his arm. He turns to look at her.

"Mariano," she whispers. She's backing away from him. "What have I done?"

"What's wrong," he tries to say, but he can't get the words out. He feels short of breath. His chest heaves as he struggles to take in air.

He turns back to the mirror and catches his reflection. He sees the unusual swelling on his abdomen. The flesh has more than filled out, it is distended, bulging and, somehow, *active* beneath the skin.

He recognizes the site, the location of his primary tumor. Her miraculous blood that restored him to vitality has shifted his cancer into overdrive. He sees the skin draw taut, feels the pressure mount. The pain is unbearable. He grabs his swollen gut with both hands, trying to hold it in, force it down. For a moment he thinks he succeeds. Then he hears the sharp, shooting crack of his ribs splintering, feels their fractured ends digging into his flesh like the claws of a predator, and he learns what unbearable really means.

The pain drives him to his knees, arms dangling useless at his sides. He remembers the doctor saying his cancer had metastasized, spread to his lymph nodes. His neck stiffens; he can't look down. It's a blessing. He doesn't have to watch as his belly splits like an overripe tomato, spilling a seething black mass between his legs.

Mariano's lymph nodes begin to burst, like enormous blackheads squeezed between a giant's fingers, spraying pus and blood and black pulp the consistency of fine caviar.

The cancer races through his veins like fire chasing gasoline, feeding on his blood. He can't breathe at all now. He welcomes unconsciousness and death, but they refuse to come.

Forever, he thinks.

He tries to move his lips in silent prayer. Please, God, no. He no longer knows if he even has lips.

He still has ears. But all he can hear is the sound of Lia's screams.

THE SOLUTION

by

Michael S. Collins

I hear you've been asking everyone what their worst experience on the job was. So I suppose it should be no surprise you've finally asked me. I wasn't too keen on the sharp end of business. I much preferred the one to one cut and thrust of human interaction. However, in a recession, a job's a job. I tried working at a call centre, but the line operator was insistent on success ("I want bites!") and the job ran at inconvenient working hours. Jobs are always after folk who can run the graveyard shift, as they call it.

My CV also had long gaps in it, which was an impediment in the current climate. Luckily, I was able to grab this occupation, going door to door to raise awareness for a good cause. Chugging, I believe it is called. I was quite good at that. And thanks to knowing one or two of the right faces in government, I was able to be called an essential service, and continue working during the recent pandemic. It's not what you know, it's who you know. Although both didn't harm.

So yes, my job involved walking down endless streets, knocking on doors. "Hello, may I come in and tell you about our latest offer?" Usually those who wanted to hear more didn't put up a struggle, and those who weren't interested you could tell a mile away. Still, on I pursued, street by street, all in the name of a fashionable cause. People like their charities to be ones they've heard of, you see.

And so, one night I was having a miserable ratio for bites, which is when people agree to be seen by you. Not a single welcoming face on the entire miserable street. You have to work up some sort of solution for getting inside their minds. It was getting late, I was getting hungry and about to head into town for a quick bite to eat, when I came to the final building on the street.

It was three storeys tall, recently built, garish and, yes, student accommodation. It was one of those buildings with the outside tannoy system that linked to a bored minimum wage guy on night shift on the ground floor, with the actual students in dorms up out of the way. I pressed the intercom button and eventually heard a bored voice.

"What do you want?" The man sounded tired as the grave.

"I'm here on behalf of charity. May I come in?" I said.

A sigh on the other end of the intercom.

"Sure, why not."

The door buzzed open and I slipped inside the building. That was the hard part done. Next I went over to the desk. The guy was alone, in an unironed security uniform, with a portion of half consumed curried chips on his desk, and instead of paying attention to his CCTV screens, had his eyes on *What We Do in The Shadows* on a small TV. The smell of the chips, already nearly off in the fully heated room, was overpowering. I really needed to eat soon. He saw my look and said, "Fancy a chip?", which was very kind of him. So I grabbed the guy by the throat, stuck my fangs in, and began drinking. At this point, you tend to get two basic reactions. "Oh shit!", and "Bugger, I knew there was a catch." That's the main problem, looking as I do, most 21st century humans are on the ball and don't want to invite me into their homes. Thank goodness for intercoms.

Chug, chug, chug, I drank.

Now the etiquette is to only drink as much as is necessary, the standard ratio of which is roughly enough to keep a human alive and well in a few days. Unfortunately for this chap, and I am rather ashamed here, I hadn't eaten in some time, and so before I knew it, I had drained his entire essence like a greedy vulture. "I'm very sorry about that," I added as I carefully lay his corpse down on the desk. I turned off the TV, too. I'm not a fan of fictional vampires. They're always fighting werewolves. As you can see, I'm mostly fighting common courtesy.

And now, it was like being the kid in a candy shop. Alone with all that young blood. A delicious nibble here or there on the first floor. This time I was more careful, so as to not wake up my food, and to make sure they would rouse later on, nary the knowledge of it. Bite marks you say? They look like insect bites, we all get them and no one notices, and does anyone really perceive being more tired than usual on a morning in the rat race? I think not.

It wasn't until I reached the second floor that the problems started. First door on the right, I entered the room. It was small and dark and instantly I got the impression I had made a mistake. I nearly did the floor below when I could tell one of the rooms had more than one occupant enjoying mutual company, but I avoided that room. But here I had walked right in… on an insomniac. He was watching BBC News on a laptop, and his head turned to the door when it opened.

"Who are you?" he asked.

From the sound of his heartbeat, I made him out to be 19 years old, Scottish, asthmatic, surprised, and slightly pissed off. I got the last three from the tone of his voice.

"I'm a chugger," I said, and you must realise by now this was the truth.

He took one look at my appearance.

"So, you're a vampire, then?"

I was taken aback. I'd have looked in the mirror to see what told him, if I could look in a mirror.

"What makes you say that?"

He made this funny sound that was halfway between a snort and a nervous laugh. "You have fangs, your shirt is covered in blood, you have a slightly decomposed face, and fresh soil on your trousers as though you kicked out of a grave."

It was my time to sigh. Carmilla was right, I was long overdue for plastic surgery!

I was getting tired, dawn was clearly due.

"If you don't mind," I said, "I'd quite like to just have a quick bite."

His response threw me. "I would mind that quite a bit, actually."

Not to worry, I was faster than him, but as I dived across the room to grab him, he added the phrase which completely shook me.

"I never gave you permission to enter my room."

Stopped mid-flight, the worst fangblock we can hear.

I sat down on his bed, confused.

"But I got permission to enter this house. From the dead guy downstairs."

He looked confused.

"Oh, he wasn't dead at the time," I added to try and be more clear.

The young student was clearly thinking on his feet, and I wondered what he studied at the university.

"You got permission to enter the building," he said, "not the house. Under the terms of my lease, this room is my own for the semester. So by law, this room is my house, not the university's. And as such, you need my permission to be here."

I felt faint in the face. Did he have a point? He began to click on his laptop before bringing up a webpage and beckoning me over to look. Student Tenancy Rights. It seemed he was bang on, and I had made a terrible mistake. With a scream, and a rush of logic, I exploded out of the room and the building before anything could take revenge. Deep gulping breaths in the cool air. Undone by a law student after 700 years. I was undone by his solution to the problem.

Oh well, at least some bites were had.

I knocked on his window one last time. He looked out of it, but didn't open it up. I was floating in the air outside.

"You made a good point," I said. "You can tell me all about this. May I come in?"

And he shot me a filthy look and said, "What kind of fool do you take me for?"

"Good Lord!" I exclaimed.

"Which Lord?" he asked.

"Dracula," I snarked, and sank to the ground level. In reality it was a turn of phrase from when I wasn't dead from the brain down.

Anyhow, you know how the story went next. Call to the police about the dead security guy. Armed response team with stakes at the ready trapped me between Bridge Street and a dead end. Put in an isolation unit to avoid sunlight, and the lawyer took a plea bargain. And so, here I am, in for life at Barlinnie. Well, a full life tariff might be difficult, but the Justice Minister said I was getting released over his dead body, and one day that will be a reality. We both know that. Not that I am in any hurry to get out of here, you see.

I did say I was considered an essential service in these pandemic times, didn't I? How to win friends and influence. Get a job at a call centre, memorize the landline numbers. Check them off the postcodes for home addresses. Look up the local MP. Visit them. Mesmerize them. Use them as a gateway drug into their party and government. It's all very simple. Anyone with my powers could get on their bike and look for food.

No, I mean it, I'm not in any hurry to leave at all.

After all, did you know that in a prison no one has any rights? You have a cell to live in, but they are not your house. In fact, once you are invited inside, that counts for your entire prison visit. And so I can move as freely as I wish. If I'd thought of this sooner, I'd have got a life tariff *all-you-can-eat* sentence centuries ago. Far easier than walking the streets desperate for a chugger.

You see, the prison system is desperately overcrowded at the moment. And I.... I am the solution.

WHAT LITTLE REMAINS

by
Paul Alex Gray

Murns in the morning, dressed in in of a child. From the nt window, I watch him skipping along the street. He flashes a smile at me through the glass as he leaps over the tumbled-down fence. The crows in the dead maple flap and slink away into the murky sky.

Inside he struts around in a disturbing charade before jumping up on the couch. He makes loud noises that sound nothing like a child, and he kicks the cushions to the floor. He falls to his belly and places his hands beneath his chin, gazing at me with hollow eyes.

“I wasn’t hungry, but I couldn’t resist,” he says.

He’s kicking his feet lazily, back-and-forth.

“Children are always the best,” he says, sucking on his fingers before laughing.

I want to turn away, but he holds my gaze.

“You used to love stealing,” he whines. “You’re no fun anymore.”

Then he straightens up and closes his eyes. Still smiling, he raises a small hand, and a long dark claw pierces his index finger. He stabs it into the place where his neck meets his chest and he tears downwards. Beads of blood erupt, and he tears off the skin, leaving it in a steaming heap by my chair.

Free of his disguise, he swirls in the hallway. His true form is a smudge of grey *not-light*. His eyes, black slits, glare for a long moment.

He slips into the den and the lock clicks.

I curse him under my breath and sit in the still room, waiting for the voice to come. Skins carry remnants of souls. If I listen carefully, I can hear them whispering in fear and confusion.

Momma.

I resist it as long as I can, but eventually I clutch the skin and cradle it close. It's fresh and carries the copper tinge and slickness of blood. My body tingles and buzzes. My claws edge through my fingertips. A deep sensation that might once have been hunger crawls through me. I want to slip my arms within the sleeves, dip my head and pull the child's face over my empty space. I want to breathe in the scents and memories. Perhaps I could pull some dreams and thoughts from the layers of fat underneath each freckle.

Stupid idea. There's no point getting to know these remnants. Marcus tells me that we must regard them the same way they look at a steak.

I place the skin on the faded couch and move to the bathroom. I stare into the mirror and slip a claw into my own skin, just beneath my throat. I tear down and peel myself open. In the half-light my black slit eyes stare back.

I am a monster made of smoke. A nothingness that only steals.

I've fallen in love with the girl next door.

Her name is Vanessa and she is twenty. She lives with a boyfriend who peddles drugs and keeps her well-supplied. When I first saw her, I wore a young woman's skin I took long ago, whose whispers are nothing more than a rustling of leaves.

I told Vanessa that my name is Rachel.

Some nights we go outside in the winter chill to stare at the woods behind the apartments. We sit on the brick fence behind the apartment that overlooks the bare arms of the trees. She chain-smokes cigarettes and tells me how different this place is in the fall. Every tree wearing beautiful sleeves of rust, amber and bronze. She thinks the light that slips between the branches is the physical incarnation of the sun, spilling to the earth like gold.

She tells me that she once was a singer. When I ask how a person stops being a singer she just smiles and touches my hand.

It's dangerous to meet with her. Marcus would disapprove. Friendships with humans are forbidden. Something more would be unthinkable. He'd kill her just to hurt me. I shouldn't get to know her more and put her in danger. I know this, and yet...

When I try to shake her from my thoughts, she lingers in every sight and sound.

She is not well. She's not the type that Marcus would take. The pinpricks and stains up her limbs mean her skin would taste sour, the words within scattered and broken.

But I can fix her.

She always smiles when she speaks, even though her teeth are yellowed and chipped.

I never say much. I'm not sure what to say.

After being with her I try to remember my life before, although most of what that used to be is long gone. Marcus likes to keep me lost in mystery. When I ask if we are monsters, he laughs but he doesn't answer. He tells me different things. Sometimes he claims that he bound me in a great city. Other times, he points at the stars and says we come from impossibly far away.

When I try thinking of the past, I imagine a hollow in an old tree. There is a space in the darkness where limbs and faces and places must have been. A shape that once was.

What filled it? Was I old? Young? Did I have someone?

Who made Marcus? Is he the first, or are there others like us?

I've given up on pressing him to tell me more. Even when he's in a good mood – high in some new victim's skin – he gets angry when I pester. He tells me to stop overthinking things and to thank him. Sometimes he can be furious, and he hurts me, reminding me that I belong to him.

Other times he makes me sit beside him, and he runs his claws over me. He tells me we have a gift – we can be anything and anyone. What more could you want?

Vanessa and I dream up a plan. She wants to get away and get clean, and a new beginning will make that possible.

She's writing a story and she wants me to be part of it.

We're going to escape together. She has an aunt out west who would let us stay a while. It's a small place, in a village along the coast road. She visited when she was little. The sand is grey and the waters are cold, but there are mountains that clutch at the sky, and the sunsets are to die for.

She shows me a worn out leather purse that she hides in a log in the woods. She has forty-six dollars in grimy green bills. She asks me if I have anything, and I nod and promise to bring it to her. She holds my hand and the hairs on my arms rise.

That night I go to the den, half-lit by the light that cuts through slatted blinds. The scent is thick and heavy, musty with unique hints that waft as I shuffle through the skins.

My movements wake them. They feel me and it sets them to talking. They're confused, of course. Lost. No one expects to have their insides swallowed away and have a soul-stained skin be all that's left.

Their trembling words reach out.

Who's there?

I need to get home. My wife will be waiting.

I'll kill you. I swear I'll kill you.

Please. Please, help me.

The sensation within me burns, that yearning to feel something new. I dig out an old one from the bottom of the pile, a thin old woman I took months ago. Marcus had sneered in disgust when I hobbled in. I slip myself within her and listen to the lingering words. She speaks a language I don't understand, and I wonder who – if anyone – she may be calling for.

I check the clothes and shoes and possessions piled in the corner. Rings and keys and wallets. Phones long silenced despite a thousand missed calls.

Our collection has grown large. Soon Marcus will declare it's time for us to leave. Sticking around too long draws attention. We'll abandon this place and make our way to the dead outskirts of another huge city and start a new spree.

I find a man's wallet, deftly skipping past a photo of three children. I don't know how, or even when, but somewhere along the way I made myself ignore these. I find some cash, more than enough to take Vanessa and me away.

"Sifting through old memories?"

I cry out and look back in the darkness. A tall man stares at me, long haired with half a day's stubble. Blood stains his shirt.

"This one was stronger than I thought." Marcus lets a claw out to take it off.

"Might be time to move on."

He tosses the skin by the pile. The carpet blossoms red beneath it.

I walk through the still rooms of the apartment. It's dark outside, but Vanessa wanted to leave early, before her boyfriend wakes. Marcus left last night and shouldn't be back for a day or two.

I pass the den. I should say farewell to the skins.

I stand there in the half-light for a moment, straining against the silence. Then I extend my claws and reach back, digging into my neck. I let the old woman's skin slip free, and as it falls to the floor my smoke spills out. I move to the pile, reaching tendrils in and between every crease and fold.

I can sense them all. I've worn each one. I've used them to do terrible things. Each one a victim, but through my actions, a murderer, also. The memory of each moment swirls in my mind, the lust for blood and the taste of souls. An addictive bitterness. An endless loop of guilt.

I withdraw and pull on the skin that I hope will be Rachel forever. I go to the bathroom and flick the light, staring at my deep brown eyes. I wash my face and pull my hair back. I open my mouth and look at the slight gap between my front teeth. I poke out my tongue, pink and healthy. I feel my naked body, touching the curves and indentations, parts soft and hard.

What will happen when we stop to eat or sleep? I'll have to tell Vanessa. Show her what I really am.

Then when I grow hungry, when I need to wear a new skin, what then?

Would I tell her what I've done in the past? All the people I've killed.

Could she be with a monster?

No. She could not. No one could. I'll have to hide it.

I shake the thoughts from my mind and get dressed quickly, then turn off the light and walk to the front door. I cast one last glance through to the den, then step outside and shiver in the chill.

I wait by the apartment stairwell, listening as the wind makes the tree branches hum and tosses leaves around.

There is a sound of footsteps, and Vanessa spins towards me, flashing a smile.

"Ready to go?" she whispers.

She touches my shoulder for a moment and a light flares inside – so bright and strong that my smoke shudders

I smile at her in return, picking up my pack and taking her hand.

There is a rushing sound and the leaves jump and dance in a swooping arc.

In the driveway, a shadow looms. Marcus steps forward in the bloody skin of the tall man.

Vanessa shrieks.

"You think you can leave me?" he asks.

He stalks towards us, his shirt stiff and dark with dried blood.

"Let us go," I say.

"They're just shells," he spits, and moves closer, unfurling his claws. I hiss in response, the smoke within me churning.

"I knew you were up to something, but this? You want to leave with this filth?"

"Who is that, Rach?" asks Vanessa, backing up. She slips on the stairs and falls back.

I stand between them, my arms raised.

He laughs. "And what will you do?"

His eyes flash with hate and he moves fast, throwing me out of the way. He grabs her, lifting her in his arms, and she shrieks.

I spin and jump up. He's holding Vanessa high with one hand, the claws on his other extended, black and bright. He cuts her scream short as he pierces the place beneath her neck and pulls down, blood spilling out with the smoke and substance of her soul.

He opens his mouth and drinks.

My own smoke burns hot inside me, spilling out from my mouth and eyes. I'm boiling within and the world shudders and cracks.

I draw in behind him, extending my claws. I jam them deep into the back of his neck, and he screams as I arc my hand down, tearing fabric and muscle and sinew.

He drops Vanessa and she cracks against the wall as he turns, snarling. But it's too late, my claw reaches his groin and he twists and falls to the ground.

With a hiss, I am upon him, tearing him apart, ripping him open.

His smoke, thick and hot, sparkles with light. It roars and boils in anger, and I grab Vanessa, her eyes sunken and her chest hollow.

I guide his smoke, pushing it inside her. She convulses, foam bubbling from the sides of her mouth. I force the last fragments in between her chattering teeth.

Then he is gone, the last of Marcus carried away in the wind. The tall man's skin lies empty by my feet.

Vanessa slumps in my arms and I draw the flaps of her chest together as I count the seconds. If she's taken the smoke, she might heal; but the skin remains open, flesh and smoke singed black.

The sky lightens. People will have heard the noise. We need to go.

I reach to her hair, pull it from her face. Wipe the spit from her mouth.

"Please," I say.

She is floppy in my arms, heavy and inert. I shift my leg and pull her close, kissing her temple. I shake and groan as tears burn my eyes, wanting to scream.

There were stories to come. She told me so.

I place my cheek on her forehead. I shut out thoughts that spill and tumble.

Then she shakes. Her chest glows, the skin reaching together and sealing up. She opens her eyes and stares at me. I choke and wipe my face clean, kissing her cheeks and patting her.

"What?" she asks, confused.

"Sshhh, come with me." I help her to her feet.

I'm shaking, the realization of what I've done echoing in my head. Will she be like me? If I made her, is she mine, like I was Marcus'? I help her sit against the wall, pulling her hair back from her face. I carry the tall man's skin away, tossing it in the woods.

The wind groans as I head back to the stairwell.

I take Vanessa and lead her to the street. The crows watch as we pass by the maple tree. I can think later. For now, we need to get somewhere.

I glance to the apartment and think of the den. I picture the skins and I try to imagine their whispers. Could they know? What would they say?

The sky brightens but the sun remains hidden. A line of yellow light splits the horizon above the buildings.

We hurry along, and I'm still shaking, but something within me hums. I feel my face tighten and I think that for just a moment, I might be smiling.

Vanessa clutches my hand, claws digging into my skin.

"I'm… hungry," she says.

It sounds like a command.

A FIEND INDEED
by
Nicholas Stella

MONDAY

Neville needed to be sick. He pulled the waste bin out from under his desk and got down on his knees, preparing to heave.

"Did you see him?"

He looked up at Leanne from Accounts. She was a little dumpling of a woman with a large mole on her chin that irked him. "What?"

"The new manager," she said. "He just arrived."

"Do you mind?" Neville didn't often speak more than one word at a time to Leanne. It wasn't just the mole that annoyed him. It was the high-pitched voice and her constant talk of cats. But mostly it was the mole.

"He's gone into the office," she said in a whisper as if it were a matter of national importance.

Neville stood and grasped the cubicle wall, tasting bile at the back of his throat. The door to the manager's office was shut and the blinds on the window were down.

"He was very tall," she said. "He had to duck to get through the doorway." She leaned in closer, her chins wobbling. "And I think he was wearing a cloak."

Neville sat back down and Leanne wandered off.

'A cloak?' he thought. 'Another lunatic is just what we need around here.'

He made a few sales calls, trying to ignore his nausea. He hadn't been having much luck this month in the sales department. What did he know about liquid soap anyway?

Neville's mouth was parched. He shuffled across the room, past his colleagues in their cubicles, to the water cooler. A change in manager couldn't have come at a better time, he thought. Mr. Crafter, the previous big wig, had been gunning for his dismissal.

"Hey, Nevster!" Warren from Marketing was filling a cup.

Neville clenched his fists at the greeting.

"Seen the new head honcho?" his colleague asked. Warren was in his late thirties, single and had a moustache to cover his cleft palate scar.

Neville shook his head, took a cup and filled it to the brim.

"Tall dude. Wears a cloak."

Neville drained the cup. "Bye, loser," he mumbled and dropped the cup in the bin.

Warren laughed and patted him on the back.

He made his way back across the office, bumping into Leanne along the way.

"I've been called," she said, "to a meeting with Mr. Dark."

"Tell him about your cats," he said, and headed back to his desk for an afternoon of cigarette breaks and the occasional sales call.

TUESDAY

Neville, wearing sunglasses, had his head on the desk. His temples were pounding from the night before. Too much beer and not enough sleep.

Standing with a groan, he shivered and put his jacket on, walking across the office. Leanne wasn't at her desk and Warren didn't show up at the water cooler.

He went into the bathroom and splashed water over his face. There were dark circles under his blue eyes and the growth of stubble had taken away the sharpness of his goatee.

The door opened and Vernon from Client Support walked in, pushing the door open with a tissue in his hand. He discarded the tissue with a sneer, turning on the hot tap. "This place is disgusting," he said, pumping pink soap the colour of cake icing into his hand.

"What's that?" Neville had found a grey hair in his beard and was trying to pluck it with his fingers.

"Never mind," Vernon said, working up a furious lather under the steaming water. "Have you met Mr. Dark yet?"

"No," Neville said as he pulled the grey free.

"Is that right?" He smirked. "I'm scheduled to meet with him this morning. I'm anxious to share with him my ideas on growing the business."

Neville left the bathroom without a word. The door to the manager's office was shut and the blinds were drawn. Arriving back at the cubicle, he slipped his glasses back on. He dozed on and off throughout the afternoon and left early.

WEDNESDAY

Neville had stayed away from the pub the night before and had enjoyed a good sleep. The races were on today so he needed a clear head to place his bets.

He walked past a number of empty cubicles, dropped his bag on the desk and went to see Sarah from Finance who had only started at the office a few weeks ago. He could tolerate Sarah, as her sense of humour was a black one, and she seemed to care even less about the place than he did.

"Hey, Sarah.Where is everyone?"

"Sick?" she said, without looking up from her mobile phone.

Neville scanned the office. "Fifteen people sick? That's a lot even for this place."

"Maybe they just couldn't be bothered."

She was a decent sort, he thought, but went a bit heavy on the eyeliner.

"Good morning, Mr. Dark," a voice said.

Neville looked over his shoulder. The door to the manager's office was open and Susan from IT was shaking hands with someone inside.

He walked over, keen to lay eyes on Susan's backside, but she disappeared inside and the door shut. The door seemed discoloured, a little darker than the wall around it. He checked his watch and returned to his desk, planning on waiting for Susan to come out. He opened the newspaper to the form guide, plugged his headphones in and waited for the racing programme to begin.

By the time he was up a few hundred dollars, Neville was feeling like lunch. On the way out, he passed Susan's cubicle but she wasn't there.

"Sarah," he called, "you see Susan come out?"

"I'm not her minder," she called back.

Neville had a long pub lunch and returned to his desk to listen to the next few races. He didn't bother to make any sales calls.

By mid-afternoon, he had lost all of the money he had made. He stood and stretched, yawning as he did so. Sarah was leading two police officers across the floor to Mr. Dark's office. She knocked and the door opened.

"Good afternoon, officers," came a deep, rolling voice. "Do come in."

"Sarah," Neville called out in a hoarse whisper.

She strolled over looking as if she was stoned.

"What's going on?" he asked.

"With what?"

"The police. What do they want?"

"None of my business."

"Did you see him?" he asked. "Mr. Dark?"

"Yeah."

He waited for her to elaborate, but she started walking back to her desk. "Well, what does he look like?"

"Tall and bald."

"You know, I've never actually seen anyone come back out of that room," he whispered after her.

"I don't need to be any more paranoid than I already am," she said without looking back.

Neville dragged his chair off to the side of the desk so that he had a view of Mr. Dark's door. He sat for only a few minutes before it opened and the police came out.

After they had gone, Sarah began to laugh.

Neville stood and looked across at her, but Sarah's head was down. He looked around the office. It was half empty. "Bugger this," he said and went to the pub.

THURSDAY

Neville wandered in late, unsteady on his legs. He sat down, planting his head on the desk but felt nauseous. He crawled under his desk and went to sleep.

"Neville?"

He opened his eyes and groaned.

"Neville?" It was Edgar from Business Development. "Are you all right down there?"

He crawled out and stood, swaying just a little.

"You don't look so well," Edgar said, "maybe you have what's going around the office. A lot of people are absent. I tried to call Vernon at home and he isn't even answering."

"Nothing that fish and chips and a couple of seafood sticks won't fix," he said, patting the older man on the shoulder. Neville liked Edgar, a family man who didn't harp on too much about his kids.

A phone began to ring on the other side of the office.

"I think that's mine," Edgar said.

Neville was at the office exit wondering whether he should have his fish grilled or deep fried, when he heard Edgar talking on the phone.

"Yes, Mr. Dark. I'll be right in."

Neville watched Edgar walk across the office and knock on the door. It opened and he shook hands with Mr. Dark.

In his tender state, Neville wasn't in the condition to dash over to try and get a glimpse of the new manager. Besides, the first few days he'd had under Mr. Dark were the best he'd ever had. Long lunches, sleep-ins, bets on the ponies and naps under the desk seemed to be the order of the day. He put Mr. Dark from his mind and left the office, bound for the fish shop.

He stopped by the pub after lunch, not arriving back until late afternoon. The office was empty except for a rat scurrying across the floor. He went back to the pub.

FRIDAY

Neville arrived at work and stopped just inside the doorway. The office was deserted. A phone began to ring. As he got closer to his desk, Neville realised it was his.

"Neville Nobbs speaking."

"Mr. Nobbs." It was a bass voice that he felt in the pit of his churning stomach. "This is Mr. Dark."

"Oh, Mr. Dark. I…"

"I'll see you in my office presently," Mr. Dark said and the line went dead.

Neville stood, tucked his shirt in over his paunch and adjusted his tie. He rubbed a hand over his face and felt a decent growth of stubble. He walked across the empty office, the only sound being the scuff of his shoes.

Sarah was standing beside the water cooler, mascara running down her face.

"Are you all right?" Neville called.

Sarah didn't respond.

"I'll be out in a few minutes," he said. "We can talk if you like."

He turned from Sarah and knocked at the manager's door. It seemed to have some sort of mould growing across its surface.

It opened and Mr. Dark was standing before him. "Good morning, Mr. Nobbs. Thank you for being so prompt."

The man filled the doorway. He was much taller than Neville and his stomach seemed abnormally distended. He was backlit by a gentle light so Neville found it difficult to discern his appearance, though he seemed to be clad in a black suit.

He extended a large fleshy hand which Neville shook. The skin was cold and the fingernails were long and dirty.

"It's good to finally meet you," Neville said, feeling like he needed to say something.

"Likewise," Mr. Dark said. "Do come in."

The room was dimly lit by the glow of a desk lamp. The manager closed the door and sat in his chair behind the desk.

"Sit, please," he said, motioning to a chair directly across from him.

Mr. Dark regarded Neville for what must have been only a heartbeat or two but seemed like an uncomfortable amount of time. He was bald with a wrinkled forehead, had small dark eyes and earlobes that hung down just a tad lower than normal.

"You don't wish to discuss business plans with me, do you?" the manager asked. "You don't have a vision for this company, do you?"

"No, not really."

"Excellent," Mr. Dark said, leaning forward and smiling without showing his teeth. "For I am more inclined to discuss cows."

"Cows?" asked Neville, suppressing a smirk.

"Yes," he said, relaxing back into his chair. "Our bovine friends. And what would happen if they weren't fenced in."

"I suppose they'd wander off."

"Precisely. They would disappear to freedom beyond the bloody knives of the abattoir."

Neville wasn't sure where this conversation was headed.

"But you and your kind," he said, leaning so close that Neville could smell the rankness of his breath, "continue to return day after day to this place, my holding pen without a fence."

Neville massaged his temples. "I'm lost," he said.

Mr. Dark rose from his chair, rounded the desk and stood behind him. "Animals can sense when death is imminent," he whispered. "Did you know that animals can scream?"

Neville swivelled in his chair and turned to face Mr. Dark. He seemed to have grown taller, standing in a stooped position with his bald head touching the ceiling.

Mr. Dark continued. "But you return, unaware of the slaughter mere steps from where you formulate business plans and make sales. Or in your particular case, from where you sleep under the desk or wager on the progress of galloping equines." He looked down at Neville, running a fat tongue over his lips.

Neville stood and backed away. "Slaughter?"

"Yes. The slaughter of Leanne who wouldn't still her tongue about her cats. Of Warren who insisted on addressing me as 'The Darkmeister.' And of Susan, who was especially tasty."

Mr. Dark was between Neville and the door.

"You're a mad man."

Mr. Dark laughed an offensive rumble that shook the furniture. "Mad man? You are incorrect on both counts."

Neville edged to the side, trying to get a clear run to the door.

"You are just like Edgar. Stoic right up until I removed his scalp like the peel from an orange."

Neville's legs began to buckle. He put his hand on the desk to steady himself.

"Are you feeling poorly, Mr. Nobbs?" he asked. "Perhaps fresh air will help." He moved aside, clearing a path to the door.

With a few quick steps, Neville grabbed the handle and wrenched the door open. There was something blocking the doorway. He pushed with his palms. It was a wall of stone, black with cold water running in rivulets down its smooth surface. Neville felt a cold draught blow from the darkness at the back of the room. It smelt of blood and shit. There was also the echo of dripping water.

"I apologise," said Mr. Dark. "My joke was in poor taste." His smile was an obscene parody of mirth.

Neville backed away from the blocked door.

"I shouldn't toy with you, Mr. Nobbs, but I do so enjoy the smell of your fear." He approached Neville, running his long fingernails over the surface of the desk. "I am in somewhat of a situation, as my current aide has been displeasing me with her errant ways and poor choices. I would appreciate it very much if you would act as her replacement."

"By doing what?" Neville put his back to the wall and began to edge away.

"Gone are my days of stealth, pursuing prey down misty laneways and crouching on roof tops with the moon at my back. Now I have my prey come to me." He stepped forwards, revealing a set of black and decaying but still very large teeth. "Your role will be to scout locations for me, preferably those with the unattached, the lonely. I don't enjoy calling attention upon myself."

"Do I have a choice?"

Mr. Dark came closer.

Neville felt unbalanced and dropped to the floor.

"Engagement in servitude to me will have its occasional delights," he whispered. A fat grey tongue, like a piece of rank flesh, moved across his rotten teeth. He laughed, deep and low, and opened the door. Fluorescent light flooded into the room. "Miss Wilkshire. Please join us," he called.

Sarah entered the room, mascara running in black streaks down her cheeks. “I’m sorry,” she mouthed to Neville.

Mr. Dark’s fist struck the side of her head with a force that threw her into the wall. She fell to the floor, staring at Neville with glassy eyes.

The door slammed shut and Mr. Dark got down on his knees, slowly and carefully, and began to dismember Sarah with his bare hands.

Neville crawled away into the darkness, listening to his master grunting in satisfaction as he fed.

THE SUN SETS NONETHELESS

by
Priscilla Bettis

B ne cornfields, dense clouds block ern horizon, but the sun will set ess. My face itches for lack of a shave. Ain't no one else left, so I don't bother.

I drag one of Opal's kitchen chairs outside and park it over the sticky blood on the back porch. There's a good view of the crops back here, so none of them fanged creatures can sneak up on me. Opal prettied up the dining set only last week, and the Windsor chair wears a fresh coat of daffodil-yellow paint. Opal would have a fit, me dragging it out here, but she ain't around no more to say. In fact, it's her blood, mixed with little Owen's. If there be a God, some creature blood is in there, too.

Overhead, a murky August sky presses down on the fields and on our farmhouse and on my very being. It's humid and warm. A breeze rolls in from the northwest, teasing me with the promise of cooler weather.

Leaning forward, elbows on knees, I fiddle with the crossbow one more time. The retention spring has gone cockeyed since I last used the weapon, but if I can get the sight mount off, I can bend the spring back into place. None of my allen wrenches fit the socket, so I try the tip of my pocket knife. Too curved.

Finches patter and dance amongst the summer blossoms of our linden tree, carrying on as if all's well. Them fool birds ought to know better 'cause Opal ain't been around to fill their feeder. Owen ain't been shooting BB's at them, neither.

I lift my binoculars and look southwards long and hard at the windbreak across the way, attempting to spot the blue creatures in the shadows of the cedars. Nothing yet.

Back working on the crossbow, I try my flat head screwdrivers. Too big, the lot of them. Finally, an idea hits. I get a ballpoint pen and pull out the tip, tossing it aside and keeping the plastic grip. With my lighter, I heat the pen grip to soften it up, then jam it into the hex socket. The pen cools, a perfectly-shaped tool. I unscrew the sight mount, my fingers working with more energy now, more hope. When I take out the spring to bend it back into shape, it snaps in two.

Opal, she helped me count the bipedal beasts—there's a couple dozen left now, hiding in the windbreak—and we started naming them, too. Sky, for the color of his skin; Fatso, Navy, Treetop, Knockers, Scarface, Toothpick . . . .

I wanted Opal to stay safe inside with Owen, but she said with the two of us fighting, we could hold them off 'til help got here. I was wrong about Owen being safe. Opal was wrong, too.

All I have left then is my Winchester. My brother over in Topeka gave it to me Christmas last. Is he still alive? If he is, he's fighting just as hard as I am. Opal left me nine rounds which ain't enough, but it'll have to do.

They got Owen first, dragged him right out of his bedroom window 'bout five a.m. when the sky was pink and we'd almost made it through the night. They tossed my boy, his little arms pinwheeling midair, into the back yard. Owen's head hit the ground first, or else he would have been conscious when Scarface and another creature ripped open his torso with their toothy mouths and drank from the surging blood that filled his exposed chest cavity. I took out the two assholes mid-slurp with one arrow after another, but more creatures took their place. Using the rifle, Opal made quick work of the three that rushed her as she fought to get to her son.

The blood in Owen's open chest stopped welling. Owen was dead. The creatures guzzling my son's blood ceased drinking and backed away.

Opal turned 'round and looked at me with wide eyes. "If the blood—" She pointed at Owen's body while a sob strangled her words. "They don't feed," she finally managed.

I let an arrow rip over my wife's shoulder and nailed the bastard whose fangs were coming on fast. She spun and fired off a well aimed round herself, and I thought she'd make it back to me, but Treetop and Navy knocked her down. Opal flipped the rifle and pushed the muzzle under her chin, but before she could pull the trigger, the beasts had her supine with her chest popped open like a living autopsy. By the time I nocked the next arrow, she was dead.

I carried the bodies of my wife and son onto the porch and cleaned them off best I could. Seemed like the right thing to do before putting them to rest side-by-side under the linden tree.

I see movement and grab the binoculars. A bald, denim-colored head ventures out from under the cedars and into the waning daylight. The creature turns its black eyes upward, and its bloodthirsty fangs gleam white in the overcast day. The creature cringes and retreats, too bright yet.

Eight rounds, truth be told, because I finally figured out what Opal was trying to say. The ninth round is special.

The creatures—blue, like I said, with big-ass mouths and vocalizations that sound like a tractor pump moving congealed oil—drink at night. Daytime is my safety, but the sun is setting nonetheless.

The temperature plummets as the cold front blows in like a chilly slap to my testicles. I fight off a shiver.

Minutes rush by, and several creatures try this time. Test the daylight, cringe and retreat, test, retreat. They're like little kids at the beach, braving the water's edge, then running back to safety with each advancing wave. Except the creatures ain't kids, and they ain't little. They're a good seven feet tall and move like shadows that twitch and lurch over rough terrain. They don't hear good, I think, 'cause they got pea holes for ears. But they can surely smell 'cause they got snouts like hound dogs.

"They must have visited our planet before," Opal had said. "Where else would all our vampire literature come from? Vlad the Impaler was just a human being, after all." She was smart that way, my Opal.

I let go of a long-held breath, and it's like blowing out another candle that's been lighting the day. The sky turns from cloudy gray to the mauve of dusk, and the birds abandon their waltz and the linden blossoms for hushed safety under the eaves. I reckon the birds know better after all.

The fanged creatures advance, their war cries like a dozen tractors screeching. Each creature drops out of sight whenever it cuts across a furrow. Together, the horde looks like cornflowers bobbing up and down on a windy day, and I go ahead and laugh 'cause it might be my final chance for levity.

I trade the binoculars for the rifle and train my scope on Fatso. The skin covering his head is so smooth it looks wet. Not only was Opal a might smarter than me, but she was also a better shot. She would have taken it already, but I wait 'til the bastard gets closer, 'til I'm sure.

As soon as his shiny dome fills my magnified view, maybe seventy yards out, I pull the trigger. For a moment it looks like Fatso has a third eye where I put a hole in him. Then he drops.

"One," I say.

Sixty yards. I take out four more in succession.

"Two, three, four, five."

I load the last four rounds and slam the bolt closed. Then, the satisfaction of ripping a hole clear through Treetop's neck.

"Six, you son of a bitch, for my Opal."

Their screeching intensifies. Seems I've riled them up.

A gust hits the tree so hard that white petals streak past like Midwestern falling snow.

I wait. Forty yards out now.

"Seven."

The sky darkens by the second, and the blue of their bodies morphs with the shadowed field. It's hard to aim. I fire one off anyway.

"Eight."

I turn the muzzle around like Opal did because now I know what she meant. *If the blood don't flow*—I grin at the remaining beasts—*they don't feed.* Another blast of wind, this one bringing grit from the fields, and I squint against the dusty gale. I pull the trigger, and the sun sets nonetheless.

FINCH
by
James Pyne

The boy in the bomber jacket darted toward me screaming the name Santiago over and over, the night air carrying his voice far. If he only knew not so long ago, I was much worse than the monsters he was running from. My high cut boots clacked on the concrete pier at a fast pace. Fog rolling in from the harbor. The cruise ship *Posedia* next to me, long ago abandoned during the Second Great Depression. *Homeless Haven* spray-painted in shaky blue along the hull. By the sounds of the blood curdling screams coming from all over the ship, it was going to be a long night.

This was Finch's doing. Damn my feathered pet and its insatiable hunger. It was my fourth cleanup of the night thanks to Finch's vindictiveness. My long trench coat dripped blood from the last purge of newly turned that had been swarming the warehouse behind me. Thirty-seven infected in various stages of conversion.

"They killed Santiago," the boy of about 12 hollered, his long hair bushed out and frizzy. I had no idea who Santiago was. The boy almost latched onto me until noticing the blood all over my clothes. The horror on his face from the realization of what the red stuff was. "We need to get out of here. They'll kill you, too. They don't care about women or kids. They'll eat everything."

He pulled at my coat sleeve.

I showed enough of my fangs to scare him off. It was for his own good. I had no time to babysit. I had to stop this from spreading. People fear a zombie outbreak when they should dread a vampire one. Responsible vampires like myself were the only thing keeping that from happening. Finch didn't see the ramifications of his selfish actions.

"If every human is dead or converted," I said to Finch, who whizzed about the heads of the new vampires along the pier like an annoying oversized mosquito. "Tell me, Finch, what will we feed on?"

Finch pretended not to hear me as he speared through the face of one the newly turned, splitting its head open, one side falling away. The rest of its body collapsed, tripping other newly turned that were going at each other. This early in maturity, vampires were primal and territorial. In a couple of months, they would conclude it was better to get along and hunt in packs. They wouldn't live that long to come to that conclusion.

The black plumage of my pet made it hard to see him at night. His red-streaked yellow beak was the first thing his victim would see coming at them, then those beady black eyes reflecting moonlight. Before impact with my face, Finch stopped a few feet from my grasp, flapping and chirping up a storm. Over the years I've learned his language. He was scolding me for going soft and being selfish for not thinking about his needs.

The brat darted from view before I could lunge ahead and snatch him midair.

"I know what you're up to," I shouted. "It won't work."

The copperish scent of blood was heavy in the air, tempting me. Finch had enough of mercy killing. He wanted to go back to the old diet of anything goes. Though conversion to immortality heightened his intelligence, he still from time to time acted out on his primal urges. He's been a century and counting work in progress. I was the only chick with a vampiric pet for good reason; animals didn't make good bloodsuckers, too much trouble. But most nights I enjoyed Finch's company more than I would someone more like me.

The fangs and claws of the newly converted were infantile compared to mine, but in greater numbers they could kill me.

"I'm starting to think you hate me, Finch."

My troublesome pet landed on my shoulder, tugging at strands of my hair to join in.

"Oh Finch."

This was how it used to be. There was a time we used to cleanse cities of their homeless. In my adolescent years of vampire maturity, I believed I was doing humanity a favor while my pet and I sustained ourselves. No one cared if those on the streets went missing. At first no one noticed, and when they did, they were more concerned about what the newspapers were saying about a deadly virus killing off the destitute, leaving them wondering if they were next. The mayor of each city made it clear not to tell the city the truth, that the homeless were being massacred by an unknown group of people. Really, it was Finch and I having some old-fashioned fun. In those days I reveled in playing with my food and leaving a mess for everyone to see. I'm much more discreet these days. Well, apart from tonight.

"You don't play fair, my feathery friend."

He kept tugging away at my hair.

I looked back to see the boy watching from a distance along the lightless promenade. To the human eye the boy would be hidden in darkness from this distance; to mine, he was shades of dark blue and black set against a similar colored background of the condemned warehouse that I just cleansed. It was where the homeless waited for an empty bed to be available in the luxury cruiser. The left of the boy's chest radiated and pulsated red energy. It was how I could tell my kind apart from the mortals.

"If one of these slips through," I hollered to the boy, "you're good as dead. Now run."

He just stood there. Maybe he didn't hear me. I didn't have time to make things clearer. I turned back to the task at hand. One of the undead smashed out of the many windows of the cruise ship, then hopped up onto the balcony rail and leap-frogged into the starry night. Shadowed, its pale face came into view as it landed in front of me. It stood up, breathing heavy. Like all vampiric creatures, its heart pulsated in shades of grey and black energy. It showed its pitiful fangs. I almost laughed, catching myself, keeping aware of my surroundings. The other newly turned still clawed at each other but at any time they could join the one that just dropped in and focused on me.

Before I could behead it with one swat, Finch let go of my hair and spurted toward it, darting through its eye, tearing away one third of its head.

"Just like old times, then."

Only because I can't possibly hunt them all down before they scatter throughout the city like a plague. There were seven remaining, with others having slipped away in the darkness. A definite long night ahead of me.

The newly turned forgot about fighting each other over territory and focused on me. I didn't expect all of them; maybe one, but all of them? I killed anything Finch converted before they matured, so I really had no idea what they would turn out like. I just knew the longer they were alive, their pale faces melted into a ghoulish appearance. One jumped at me and I caught it by the throat, its eyes and nose leaking blood, a sure sign of a vampire that had fed too much. I slammed it down like a sack of potatoes on the concrete, stamped its face, collapsing its skull. They had been turning for a few days, living among friends and family, most likely appearing gravely ill before full conversion, then had an abundant food source trapped with them.

They pushed others out of their way to get at me first. It seemed they wanted bragging rights of taking down the queen of this city. Not on my watch. My nails stretched, a painful process earlier on in maturation, barely noticeable now. I decapitated many. Clawed their faces away, cutting through skull and brain. Punched through their chests, tore their black hearts out, still beating, and tossed them behind me into the harbor.

Finch bulleted through the chin and spurted out the back of the head of someone I recognized, an old man dressed like a sea captain. He had once been a stage actor at Bard Theatre on 6th Street. An amusing fella who always asked me for a cigarette no matter how many times I told him I didn't smoke, with him saying now was a good time as any to start. It will be the death of you, I would say, having no idea how wrong I was about my prediction. I knew most of their faces, some in passing, others through random interactions. I had been just another person to them who lived the city night life.

Finch ripped through the chest and heart of another. This was all about bringing back what Finch perceived as the golden era of our friendship, reminiscent of our biggest killing sprees during every Harvest Moon.

They crashed through the windows and rained down on us as one collective.

"You're controlling them?" I said to Finch.

It was possible. Some vampires had that ability . But a vampiric bird having such power? That was a terrifying thought. Finch killed most of those frog-leaping from every level of the ship before they landed on the pier. Severed body parts rained down. It was like Finch was unleashing years of frustration of living on a tasteless diet of croak, a not-so affectionate nickname for blood taken from somebody dying of natural causes. He refocused on those coming at me, bulleting through the hand of the one that tried snatching him midair, bits of flesh and finger spraying out. Finch was just showing off now, making this into a game to see who could kill the most, something we used to do back in the day.

The last of the jumpers had been felled. Now damage control began. How many had been infected in there? I walked across one of the rope bridges with wooden rungs and entered, Finch following. We would start from the lower deck all the way to the top.

We cleared each floor with some humans torn apart. Quite a few of them remained alive, their hearts beating, threads of darkness spread through the pulsating glow about their chest. How frustrated Finch was when I refused to feast on all this prime blood. Sure, it was a waste, but if I fed on such vigorous blood after all this time, I would be far nastier than Finch. I would be an addict all over again.

It was getting harder with each level, avoiding any blood getting on my mouth. Some tried standing up to me. Those with the most fire in them were the ones that tempted me the most. Blood from alpha types was like one's favorite flavored ice cream. I should go feed and come back later, long after temptation had subsided. If I did, I would return to an empty ship, and nights from now there would be pockets of outbreaks everywhere.

The last few I decapitated nearly broke me. I almost fanged their flesh, resisting with everything in me, pulling away at the last second, my mouth closing over my venomous fangs. That's where the infection usually started, from our virulent saliva that numbed our prey into submission. Only other way to be turned was drinking vampire blood.

I swiped at the last vampires standing. Its head spiraled through the air and exploded all over the place from Finch rocketing through it.

"Just like the old –"

Finch's blood-soaked plumage grazed my lips at his passing.

"Frigging brat." I wiped it away in defiance. No lies. I wanted to lick my lips so bad but if I did, more would die tonight. Lots more would. I would be totally unhinged in such a rebirth. "After all these years, you underestimate me. My will is stronger than yours."

Finch whizzed through one side of my hair. I could never kill Finch. I loved him too dearly to even entertain such thoughts. Besides, even if I wanted to, there would be no catching him. Something had to be done, though, but how do I blame him for his actions when they were learned from me? I wasn't going back to my old life.

There were some nights I wished I left him on that Galapagos island where he and his friends, other vampire finches, pecked away on the back of the heads and necks of the local booby population, lapping away on their blood. I had read about these odd creatures in Darwin's *Origin of Species*, and being immortal, I was curious to see if these mysterious birds were of the undying. They were of course not, but one of them had the audacity to land within my hair and draw blood from the back of my neck before I realized it wasn't just being playful and curious.

I had to get out of here. The scent of blood had my eyes rolling up from the ecstasy of a growing bloodlust. Too much blood scent in the air. Had to –

A shriek from someone below. Over by the warehouse I had cleansed an hour ago. The boy swatted Finch away who was playfully tormenting the kid. I jumped from the top deck, landed in a crouch, and slowly rose from the concrete pier littered with bodies and blood splatter.

"Leave the kid alone, Finch."

He ignored me, pinched the boy's hair between his beak, and pulled at it, moving this way and that, avoiding the kid's attempts to whack him.

"Finch, back off."

Finch darted toward me, making it seem like he was going for my face, then veered from that path. Landing on my shoulder, he nestled into my hair.

"You're not going to cute your way out of this."

His attempt at sad puppy eyes had me rolling mine.

Finch lifted a wing to hide his face in shame, then peeked over it.

I smirked, doing my best not to laugh, feeling wrong to do such a thing with all the innocents slaughtered. After all this, the boy refused to run off, even though it was obvious he was frightened.

"That . . . bird . . . it came at me." A bewildered look came over him. "Birds don't fly at night. And what are you? You are like them, but killed all of them."

"Every kind of life has bad apples." I glared at Finch. "I'm a vampire. Not like the movies, before you go there."

"Really? How long have you been alive?"

"We'll get to that."

He said nothing, like he just decided he would rather forget all that bad stuff that happened. He would have seen enough of it to stick with him, heard more than enough to scar him for life.

"You're brave for a boy."

"I have to be. Santiago said so. The streets aren't kind to anyone weak, that's what Santiago always said." A look of sadness came over the boy as he stared in the direction of the mostly shadowed cruise ship. No doubt he had family dead in there.

"Are you or your bird going to hurt me?"

"You would be dead if I had intent to harm you. And this here is Finch. He's forbidden to hurt kids. You know, I originally called him Nib, but he preferred the name of his species. What an ego. King of the finches. I should have known he would be trouble. I sometimes call him Nib just to annoy him."

"Nib," the kid said, smirking.

Finch chirped at the kid, hopping on my shoulder, wings flapping in a frenzy.

The boy giggled. It was nice to see, considering what just happened.

"What's your name?" I asked.

"Cade."

"I'm Cahya." I almost offered to shake his hand, remembered my claws were still partially out. They shrank back into sharp looking fingernails. "Why didn't you run off?"

"I got nowhere to go."

I had no words. Guilt flooded me. I looked down at Finch. His beaked face slowly turned away from me.

"Can I pet him?"

"He doesn't know you well enough. But you really should have run. One of them could have squeaked by."

"I knew you would protect me." He smiled at Finch. "Him, too."

Cade looked over at the *Posedia.* The quarter moon reflected off the harbor.

"Kiddo," I said, "I'm so sorry if your parents were on there."

"No, they died last year. Been on the street since. I just got in there with a friend, one like a dad to me. Santiago." He started whimpering. "They . . . they started biting him. I didn't know what to do. He screamed for me to get out of there. It didn't feel right leaving him, but they were all around us, I just started running. Then I saw you. Please don't leave me. I have no one."

If I thought I could trust Finch, I would let the boy pet him, get his mind off things. I needed to get my mind off things, too, and being around this kid wasn't helping. A breeze carried with it the scent of dying blood, still enough to have me sniff out fresher blood. I couldn't abandon Cade. Or be around him for long. Not right now. I needed to sniff out someone closer to dying than living.

Yes, that's what I would do. I would escort Cade to somewhere safe, tell him to stay there until I return. Maybe by then I would have figured something out.

He hugged me.

Damn it. I needed him to be further away from me. Not closer.

I looked up at the starry night, the quarter moon not lighting up much along the promenade. All lights had been busted out long ago.

"Promise me you won't leave me."

I didn't want to look down. Just wanted to run away, as pathetic as that was for a vampire my age to think. Another part of me felt like once I sorted things out, I could be a motherly figure to this kid. A protector. I did it one other time. A heartbreaking thing to watch them rot into old age. I could do it one more time. At least help him into adulthood, get him in a good place in life. But first this bloodlust needed quenching, I had to get away from him before —

"What's wrong?" Cade asked.

I gently pushed him away, looking down at him to assure him everything would be okay, that –

My eyes widened at the sight of the pulsating red energy over his chest, darkening in spots.

A COLD DISH

by

Lonnie Bricker

"I'm tellin' ya, they keep it in the old tunnel." Jerry ducked a branch and continued through the trees. Long shadows dappled across his back, making him vanish and reappear as if he were some sort of fae.

"They sealed that up." Chris had no trouble weaving his skinny body through the undergrowth, but his shorter legs struggled to keep up.

"Father O'Connell showed me the secret entrance." Though only birds and squirrels might overhear, he finished in a hushed voice. "Right before he did *that*."

Having *that* in common was the only reason the eight-year-old Jerry hung out with a seven-year-old.

"He didn't show me any secret entrance," Chris said.

"Probly 'cuz you'd blab. Look, it's in there all right, a real vampire. He said they use it to test priests who are gonna do hard jobs. They gotta brand it with a cross or somethin'."

"It'll eat us."

"It's chained up." Turning, Jerry pushed through a bush. "'Sides," he said over his shoulder, "zombies eat people, vampires suck blood."

"I'll still be dead!" Chris hurried to catch up.

Barely visible at first, flashes of white paint and stained glass grew larger the closer they came to their destination. Then the trees gave way to an empty gravel parking lot. On the far side sat a chapel that was old when their grandparents were kids.

"Remember," Jerry said, "we don't let it loose 'til it promises to kill Father O'Connell."

"Can it hear us? My dad said the old tunnel is under the ground over here." He pointed at their feet.

"Dunno. Don't think so," Jerry said. "They use ta hide runaway slaves in it, so I think it's soundproof or somethin'."

Chris caught Jerry sneaking a glance at the ground but pretended not to notice. Mentioning it would only make him mad.

In the clearing, the afternoon sun chased away the gloom of the forest but did nothing to dispel his fear. Never had walking across a parking lot in broad daylight been so frightening. At any moment, Chris expected to hear a car's tires crunching on the gravel lane that wound through the woods. A buzzard passed overhead. Its shadow climbed the church's wall, morphing into something out of a nightmare as it plunged over the roof. He touched Jerry's shoulder and pointed to the bell tower. "I saw eyes."

"I saw eyes," Jerry repeated in a high-pitched voice. "Ha! C'mon, ain't nothin' up there. It's just

the sun reflectin' off the bell. Father O'Connell showed me."

"Why didn't he show everyone, then?"

"Said it keeps kids from climbin' up there."

The double doors at the front of the chapel were unlocked. Inside, light filtered through the stained glass windows, painting the worship area in multihued color. Rows of wooden pews, hand-polished every six months for over a hundred years, filled the air with the aroma of beeswax and turpentine. In any other church, it would have been a welcoming, calming smell. Chris gagged.

At the far side of the room, behind the raised pulpit, a door on the right and another on the left offered access to rooms beyond. Holding onto each other, the boys tiptoed down the middle aisle. Jerry opened the door on the right and flipped the light switch. A single bulb illuminated the thirteen steps leading to the basement of the chapel.

Father O'Connell pulled the church van onto the McCall's asphalt driveway and opened the driver's side door. The grating squeal—a sound only rusty metal could make—shot through his spine and set his teeth to vibrating. Heaving his bulk from the van, he shuffled up the walk. This day had been inevitable. He knew it as surely as he knew there was a God in heaven. Unbidden, his mind envisioned all the different tales the boy might have told; then, like a defense attorney, walked through the rebuttals, each ending with a promise to pray for the child's soul. *Stop,* a voice inside his head said with a finality that halted him in his tracks. *It's bad enough you abuse the trust of God and those He put in your care. If the child has told his parents of your sins, you will do nothing to disparage him.*

Unbidden, he pictured the pretty, freckled face of Father Bowen, who had passed through a couple of weeks ago. As he did with all the eager young priests the Church sent, he had asked him to be his confessor; and like the others before, the redhead had prescribed penance in a tone reeking of suppressed disgust for the monster in the confessional beside him. It didn't matter, nothing could completely assuage his guilt, perhaps because even as he swore never to do it again, a part of him was conjuring excuses, planning for future failure. Could it be part of God's plan for the boys?

Stop.

Bowing his head, he gave silent thanks that today would be the day. Re-tucking his shirt into his pants, he double-checked the buttons hiding under his belly by touch—he'd lost sight of that area years ago.

Ben McCall answered after the first knock. His stocky figure, beer gut, and balding head were the very embodiment of the ex-jock whose glory days were a decade behind him.

"Glad you could come, Father," he said, inviting him in. The front door opened directly into the living room, where a brown fabric sofa and loveseat formed two sides of a square, with a floor model 19" television and a front bay window forming the other two. Dozens of family photos decorating the yellow walls featured Ben, his wife

Betty, and their son, Jerry. The aroma of cookies baking filled the house, embracing him with its soothing chocolate chip wholesomeness.

Ben shut the door behind them. "I'll get Jerry." He disappeared down a hallway that led deeper into the house.

Betty McCall stepped through the doorway that led to the kitchen. "Perfect timing, Father. The cookies are almost done. It's like God is on your side." She laughed at her own joke, sending her long red ponytail into a bobbing fit as she wiped her hands on her already flour coated jeans.

"You sounded troubled earlier," Father O'Connell said. "Is everything all right?"

"I'm sure it is. It's just that Jerry has been acting … odd."

"How so?"

Ben marched back in. "Jerry's gone."

"I'll call Mrs. Walker, see if he went over there." Betty stepped to a phone hanging just inside the kitchen.

"I'm sorry, Father. He was told to wait in his room. Kids these days have no respect." Ben shook his head.

"I like to imagine we've all slipped off without permission a time or two in our lives."

"I suppose, but that's no …" Ben trailed off at the sound of his wife hanging up the phone.

Betty came back in wringing her hands. "He was there, but he and Chris went to play in the woods."

A stone weighted with enough guilt and sin to crush Mother Teresa and half the saints settled on his chest—those boys were not playing in the woods. Telling Jerry had been a mistake. *Not enough to take advantage of the boy, you had to impress him, too*. "I'll help you look for them."

Ben shook his head. "No, that's okay, Father."

"It's truly fine. I need to go to the church anyway, and it's in the middle of the forest." He held up one hand forestalling the argument already forming on Ben's lips. "If I see Jerry and Chris, I'll send them home."

Back in the van, he glanced up at the falling sun and accelerated.

Jerry pushed on the leather spine of the book, depressing it like a large button. With a click, the bookshelf swung toward them. "Told ya," he whispered. "Just like in the movies." He pointed at the flashlight Chris held with both hands, its beam barely visible under the overhead lights in the basement. "Ya don't need that thing."

"I will when you open that." Chris motioned toward the door that had been hiding behind the bookshelf. It was an ancient thing made of thick wood planks bound with bands of iron. A metal ring bigger than his head hung where a doorknob would normally be.

"You ready?" Jerry grabbed the ring.

"Y-y-eah."

Jerry pulled and the door swung open on soundless hinges. The flashlight beam pierced the darkness, illuminating a portion of a long tunnel. Wooden beams the size of logs braced the walls and ceiling. Dense cobwebs filled the corners high and low. Twenty feet from where they stood, the darkness swallowed the light, leaving the tunnel beyond enveloped in blackness made more terrifying by the knowledge that a real monster waited somewhere in its depths. Chris swallowed and glanced back at the steps leading up to the house of God.

"Let's go."

Chris misunderstood and stepped back.

Jerry grabbed him by the arm. "We gotta do this. He won't stop."

Chris swallowed hard and gave a determined nod. "Okay."

When Jerry released his arm and started down the tunnel, he followed, remaining close enough that he could feel his breath rebounding off his friend's back. Peanut butter and jelly sandwiches didn't smell so good when mingled with the wet dirt odor of the tunnel.

Jerry stopped. Hanging from the top of a doorway, dusty cobwebs blocked the flashlight beam as effectively as a curtain.

"Come on." Jerry took a step forward.

Chris did, though he shook so violently the flashlight beam bounced from floor to ceiling. The cobwebs fell apart when they got close, shreds of gossamer floating to the earthen floor. "It looks like ice." When he realized he had spoken, he slapped a hand over his mouth.

"Shine it in the room."

The vampire, dressed only in a pair of baggy cargo shorts, sat on the floor at the far end of a stone room. Hissing, the lean, dark haired figure stood in one smooth motion. Metal chains that looked capable of stopping a pickup truck uncoiled from the floor in a rattling cacophony of wrist-thick links. Chris gasped; burned into every inch of flesh were raw, angry brands, each in the shape of a cross. Golden cat-eyes glinted. Muscles capable of tearing little boys apart like paper flexed and strained. Several of the fresher brands began to weep blood.

It sniffed the air, and with a snarl, curled back thin pale lips, exposing fangs half an inch long. "You are not one of *them,*" it said in a gravelly voice that brought to mind Mister Johnson, who smoked two packs of cigarettes a day.

Chris shook so violently the flashlight beam bounced from floor to ceiling.

"We," Jerry took a deep breath, "wanna make a deal."

"I do not deal with the living. I feed on them."

Chris took a step back, but Jerry grabbed his arm. "He said no," Chris pleaded, trying to pull free.

"Father O'Connell ain't gonna stop until someone makes him," Jerry insisted."You know that, just like you know we can't tell our folks."

Both boys hung their heads. They'd each tried, but something always kept the words from coming; it was never the right time, shame, fear of their friends finding out. It seemed like there were hundreds of reasons not to.

Jerry nodded and turned to the vampire. "We want you to kill Father O'Connell."

The creature's eyes narrowed until they were slits, and it quit straining against the chains. "Speak."

"If we let you go, do you promise to kill him?"

"Yes."

Jerry edged closer. "Where's the key?"

The vampire licked its lips. "There are no locks. The latches are blessed by a priest." It offered its wrists. "I will kill the priest, if you set me free."

"And promise you won't hurt us," Chris added from the doorway.

It grinned. "Smart boy. Yes, I promise not to hurt either of you."

Jerry turned and gave Chris a thumbs up sign. "Keep the light on him so I can see."

Obediently, Chris stepped closer and held the flashlight as still as his terror would allow.

Jerry undid a cross-shaped latch. "Pretty stupid vampire if that's all it took to hold ya." A nervous chuckle escaped his lips.

The vampire flexed its free hand.

Jerry released the last manacle. "Father O'Connell will be here toni—"

The vampire had Jerry by the throat, choking off his words. Chris turned to run. It grabbed his wrist. With a hiss, it hauled him into the air beside Jerry.

"You promised!" The boys shrieked in unison.

"I … don't … deal … with the living." One-handed, it brought Jerry to its lips. Jerry opened his mouth wide as if trying to scream, but no sound escaped the vampire's grip. With a brutal slash, the creature's fangs tore Jerry's throat open. Blood pumped from the wound, spraying Chris, and the vampire.

"Despicable creature," Father O'Connell said from the edge of the room.

Baring its fangs, it hissed, spraying more of Jerry's blood over Chris.

"Release the living boy." The priest's voice echoed through the room.

Chris's face bounced off the stone floor. The flashlight flew from his limp hand, sending the beam spinning crazily across the room. Moving surprisingly fast, Father O'Connell yanked him to his feet.

"Are you all right?" he asked while hurrying down the pitch-black tunnel. Chris tried to respond, but when he opened his mouth, something wet and tasting of salt fell from his upper lip into his mouth. Nausea surged, bringing with it bile that burned at the back of his throat. Light surrounded them as they entered the basement.

"Stay here." Father O'Connell sat him down on a folding metal chair.

"No!" Chris tugged at the priest's arm, fear of being left alone outweighing the man's sins.

"I'll be alright. I need to get it back into its chains."

"You are too late, priest." The vampire's voice was deeper than it had been. It strode into the light of the basement. Most of the cross-shaped brands had faded to nothing more than pale scars. It looked fuller, healthier. "You and your kind kept me weak and starved for a hundred and twenty-two years. No more."

Father O'Connell pulled a wooden cross from his pocket.

The vampire laughed. "The true believers who come to prove their faith on my weakened flesh might be able to use that cross. You are not one of them. "

Holding the cross at arm's length in front of him, Father O'Connell took a step forward. "You doubt my belief in God?" he asked. "My sins might assure that I rot in Hell one day, but I will do so in the knowledge that God is all-powerful, and that you submitted to His will this day."

Aiming for the vampire's chest, he took another step. Full of arrogance, the creature allowed the touch. Smoke rose from the fresh brand on its chest. The sickly-sweet smell of burning flesh filled the room, while its screech of unholy pain seemed to fill the universe.

"God will judge me for my actions one day, but you never will." Sincerity gave Father O'Connell's voice power Chris had never heard in it before.

Tearing loose from the object of its torment, the vampire flexed its hands, revealing claws as sharp as knives.

"In the name of God, stop!" The building shook with the power of Father O'Connell's command, and an explosion of the purest white light left dark spots clouding Chris's vision.

The vampire cringed, shrinking back against the wall and reminding Chris of a black lab he'd seen on a veterinarian show. Pressing against the chain link fence in the farthest corner of its cage, the dog had refused to make eye contact with the soft spoken doctor. She said its owner had beaten everything out of it but fear.

"Dare to threaten me again and you will beg for the flames of Hell." By using the cross like a cattle prod and drawing on God's name, Father

O'Connell directed the vampire back into the darkness and into its shackles. With the door closed and once again hidden behind the bookshelves, Father O'Connell knelt in front of Chris.

"God made His will known today. He could have allowed the vampire to kill us both. I think He was trying to teach us a lesson. What do you think?"

Tears streamed down Chris' face. He nodded.

Pulling a tissue from his shirt pocket, Father O'Connell dabbed at Chris' upper lip and nose. It came away bloody. "Did you get any of its blood on you? Did any of it get in your mouth?"

"I-I dunno. I think it's all Jer—" he burst into sobs.

Sighing, the priest reached out and stroked Chris' short hair. "You can never say anything about this. If someone else were to open that door, they could end up like Jerry."

He nodded again.

"I need to hear you say it, son. Promise me that you will never tell anyone."

"I promise, Father."

"Good boy." He patted him on the knee. "Now we need to get you cleaned up and out of these clothes."

With a touch as revolting as it was gentle, the priest helped him out of his t-shirt and shorts. "You know where the shower is. When you are done, dig through some of the clothes in the donation box and find something you can put on until we get these cleaned. We will say that Jerry ran away. He tried to convince you to go, but you got scared. You cannot tell anyone you two were here tonight ..."

Father O'Connell waited until the child disappeared into the basement bathroom before leaning heavily against the bookshelf. He took several deep breaths, feeling the cool air cleanse his lungs. His soul would not be cleansed so easily.

This cannot happen again. Strong in his conviction, he stepped away from the bookshelf. *I will leave Jerry's body. The next priest to test his faith will find it, and the Church will have no choice but to condemn me.*

POEM OF THE RIVERBANK

by
Gary Robbe

Seven miles south of Denver, along Cherry Creek, a tired man with a full pack on his back, and a walking stick in his hand, rested on a slab of concrete beneath an underpass. It was dark, but slivers of light crept through at either end. The man listened to the unraveling of the water as it rushed to the rapids not more than twenty feet away. It was a bogus moon, the man thought, as he leaned away from the ball of light that flittered toward him, soft and fragile like Chinese lanterns he had seen somewhere a long time ago. The bogus moon grew dark and large and stood in the swift but shallow water.

The tired man stood and gripped his stick like a baseball bat, ready to swing with all the might his beaten sixty-year-old body could muster. The man started to speak, but before he could, the light reached out to his throat, filling it with mud and river slime, a swelling fist forcing its way gently but forcefully, crushing his trachea and esophagus, his eyes suddenly on the trail of stars and the real moon as he was dragged into the water and out of the underpass. His last thought was how pretty the watermelon moon was.

Gerald woke early, as usual. The sun was morning dull. It was exactly seven o'clock. He removed and folded his pajamas neatly and placed them in the dresser, then put on gray sweatpants and a gray tee shirt. He brushed his teeth for thirty seconds, gargled with mouthwash, then polished the mirror where splatters of toothpaste had landed. He used the toilet, washed his hands and brushed his hair. He donned a gray sweatshirt before leaving for the river.

The South Platte River was two and a half blocks from his one-bedroom apartment in downtown Denver. A path led to the riverbank, not far from a pedestrian bridge, and Gerald followed it until he came to a bench that faced the river. In late fall and winter when the trees were bare he could see the skyline of the city, and he always enjoyed watching the soft rushing water of the South Platte. At night he sat on the bench and listened to it bubble past.

Gerald said hello to everyone he met on the path. He liked people. All people, whether they crawled out from the bushes reeking with body odor and alcohol and pot, or walked on the path wearing a Polo outfit and top end running shoes or sandals.

He noticed shoes. Make and model, how they were worn, how the person carried themselves in the shoes. He was a shoe salesman, after all.

"You can tell a lot about a person the way they walk or run in their shoes," he told a homeless man named The Sage that morning. The Sage didn't talk much, but often met Gerald at the bench in the early morning. Gerald paid attention to him and talked to him like he was a real person. The Sage liked that. Besides, Gerald enjoyed Edgar Allen Poe as much as he did, and they often shared bits and pieces of the man's writings between them.

"And by the kind of shoes they're wearing." He pointed to two young women walking the trail. "That lady's toes are going off her sandals. She needs to loosen up. And her friend's trying to impress everybody, but her cheap Adidas are wearing out on the sides."

Gerald regarded The Sage's boots, worn out, no determinable brand. "Sage, I keep telling you. Come into Macy's and I'll find you some good boots – no charge. You shouldn't wear those worn out things."

The Sage followed the early morning clouds, nodded. "You need more friends."

"Tell you what," Gerald said. "I'll pick up a pair for you." He studied The Sage's boots. "Looks like you wear a size ten."

"Shoes are fine," The Sage said. He was a short man with a droopy face, layers of clothes and coats that gave him a Quasimodo look. "Be careful, my friend. Word is out that a maniac is butchering people on the trails in Denver. Everyone is scared shitless." He shook his head. *"Sir, said I, or madam, truly your forgiveness I implore..."* He bowed and swept his greasy hands before him. *"But the fact is I was napping, and so gently you came tapping..."*

He slowly pushed the cart, overflowing with unnecessary things. *"Tapping at my chamber door, that I scarce was sure I heard you."* With a broad half toothed smile, he ambled off along the riverbank.

Gerald shouted, *"Here I opened wide the door – Darkness there, and nothing more!"*

The Sage cackled with laughter, and without turning, gave a subtle wave goodbye.

Gerald watched him go. Followed the current of the water. Noted the branches and man-made debris floating by. The water was high. It was early Spring and the trees opposite were blooming white, some of the branches stripped of flowers by the rain the night before. Petals floated by like mad teacups.

Gerald worked at Macy's in the men's shoe department. Business had been slow and usually he was the only salesman on duty. He worked from 11:00 to 9:00 every day except Thursday and Sunday. He thought of the customers who visited the store as friends, or people who could become friends.

That night, Mr. Barnes bought a pair of Hushpuppy loafers. Mr. Barnes was a friend. He reminisced about trips he had taken with his late wife. Gerald had never been out of Colorado before, and was keenly interested. He had read about many distant places, and desperately wanted to see the rest of the world. But knew he never would. Mr. Barnes was a lucky man indeed. He said so. Mr. Barnes didn't appear to appreciate the remark and left soon after.

Mr. and Mrs. Johnston, a nice elderly couple who lived in a high rise not far from Gerald, also came in and bought walking shoes. Mrs. Johnson had recently been diagnosed with cancer, and after they left Gerald was quiet with worry.

As he was straightening the boxes strewn on the floor, he overheard Mrs. Warstein, who worked in the women's clothing department, and Ted, a young college student who worked part time evenings, talking about a gruesome discovery along Cherry Creek that some bicyclists stumbled upon that day. Mrs. Warstein was upset about it, this being the third homicide in Denver this month along one of the waterways. Gerald wanted to hear more details, but was sidetracked when two young men came over, looking for running shoes.

The odor of marijuana was strong, and the men were beside themselves with the way Gerald waited on them. They giggled and almost rolled off the chairs with every polite thing he said, and when Gerald turned his back, they mocked everything he said. Gerald thanked them effusively for shopping at Macy's and for giving him the pleasure of waiting on them. When he said have a great evening, they shouted, "Have a great evening!", back to him, over and over all the way through the store and out into the mall. Ted and Mrs. Warstein laughed, but he didn't mind. The kids bought shoes and Gerald felt he gave good customer service.

He was thinking about the Denver homicides when a dark dressed stranger came in, looking for wing tips, shortly before closing. He was old, a weathered face held together with fine lines, like the minute cracks in antique porcelain, and was very thin. He moved like he weighed nothing at all.

Gerald said hello and told the man that he looked distinguished, getting a chuckle from him. He commented on the man's accent.

"Armenian," the man said. Gerald placed a handful of shoeboxes before the man, knelt down to slip off his well-worn but expensively made shoes. The shoes tingled Gerald's fingers. Static electricity, he thought.

"We don't carry anything quite like these," he said. "But the Florsheim is good. Let's see how they fit." The shoes were tight. "Armenia," he said. "I've read about that country. I've always been interested in geography." He stood. "Let me check and see if we have a larger size."

"I'm so sorry," Gerald said when he returned. He looked straight into the man's murky blue eyes. Distant eyes, ocean deep. "I can order them. They'll be here tomorrow."

"That would be fine." The man crossed his legs, content to stay awhile. "Have you worked here long?"

"I've been here forever," Gerald said. "I practically live here." He sat on the stool before the stranger, still fixed on those eyes. Gerald asked if he lived around here, he seemed new to these parts.

"You're observant," the man said. His long white hair reached his shoulder but was impeccably well placed without looking overly fashioned. "I'm new to Denver. I moved here from the coast." He went on to say how different it was compared to New York, the people more relaxed, nicer even, and the wide-open spaces. The mountains.

They talked until closing time. Gerald was polite and conversational to a fault. He loved meeting new customers and hearing their stories.

The man asked about him, where he lived, what he did when he was off work. Gerald said the store was his life, but he did like to spend time by the river. Water was magical.

"Indeed, it is." The man stood and extended his hand. Gerald took it although he rarely liked to touch people. The man's grip was surprisingly soft and cool. "Arsen," he said, introducing himself. "I enjoyed talking to you."

"I'm Gerald. Your shoes will be here tomorrow night, Arsen." He paused. "I'll be here."

The Sage stumbled on the trail, caught himself with the aid of a dead tree branch that scratched his hand, and returned upright and unsteady. He wiped his hand on a blanket in his cart, then pushed ahead down the narrow trail. The wind kicked up and scattered leaves and paper trash like ice feathers dropped from the heavens.

The Sage breathed heavy. He was tired and a little drunk and a lot cold right now, the wind slipping into every hole his clothes allowed. He cursed the night. He cursed the assholes who took his spot a mile down the river, his home, by God, the Sage's kingdom, and here he was, in the middle of the night in the dark, listening to the running water and the cackle of wind pushing against the trees and shrubbery.

Then, a soft voice. *"From childhood's hour I have not been, as others were – I have not seen, as others saw..."*

"Gerald, is that you?" The Sage stumbled off the path into the weeds where he thought the voice was coming from.

He never heard the scythe-like claws that ripped into and through his neck. Before he could gargle out a blood-soaked cry, he was falling back, and something was on him, something monstrous big. Crushing his chest, the bones crackling like a healthy bonfire. The Sage didn't feel the teeth on his ripped throat, many teeth, gnashing and tearing to get at what life force flowed out. Somewhere way distant he thought a large cat, a mountain lion, got him.

Then a sigh. No, it was the air escaping from his severed windpipe. And when all the blood and air were siphoned from his body and he knew he was dead, he heard, *"And all I lov'd, I lov'd alone."*

A dark shape hovered over the body and pulled pieces of it apart as if the Sage had always been made of malleable clay. The pieces were scattered along the woods and the easy river. The shape wiped the blood from its mouth with an arm that reached to the ground. It wobbled slightly from the gorging it had just taken.

A cloud uncovered part of the moon and light rippled on the surface of the river. The banks on both sides were overgrown with lush plant life, and there should have been the sound of crickets, cicadas, mosquito's wings, and frogs, mournful wails of night birds, the fervent rustling of rodents, but there was no sound whatsoever.

The running water was soothing, and the shape took in the neon reflections of the moon on the water's surface. The river, like all rivers, was the source of all life, of all death. Things never changed over countless centuries and new lands.

It could have walked the city streets, the many dark alleys, the secluded parks, the hallways of near empty office buildings to find nourishment, and sometimes it did. Sometimes it made a game of the hunt, selecting and seizing its prey in the most open of places, sometimes even in a crowded or well-lit department store. It was a magician at disposing bodies.

But the shape preferred rivers. For centuries it could simply follow the river and select prey and never worry about the monotony of returning to the same scene. It could move great distances, never worrying about depleting its food source. The river, rich in symbolism, the birthplace of all great civilizations, the arteries and veins of the planet.

The creature turned within itself and became a shadow that swallowed the night whole, and disappeared.

The Sage's cart took the first sprinkles of a light rain, and then the steady downpour on the side of the dirt path, the front wheels buried in weeds and mud, and only yards from the closest pieces of what was left of the Sage.

When Gerald left his apartment to visit the river, he discovered an envelope by his door. He assumed a neighbor, or the apartment manager, put it there since the building had a locked entry way. Nothing was written on it, but there was something hard inside. He opened it.

He gasped and dropped the envelope to the floor as if it had ignited in his hands. A severed finger, gray, bloodless, desiccated and dry. He pulled himself together and picked it up, studied it for a second until he became nauseous, dropped it again. His first thought was to call the police. Then the apartment manager. He thought on it, hard.

People in the building were always teasing him. It *had* to be a practical joke. *Well, I'm not going to give them any satisfaction.* He dropped it in the dumpster on the way to his usual spot near the river.

He was out of sorts all day, but didn't want to tell anyone about what he found that morning. And it bothered him that he didn't see his friend, The Sage. He tried to busy himself with straightening shoeboxes in the backroom, and every time he peeked out from the curtain all he saw was Mrs. Warstein, pacing the floor. She was angry that Ted didn't show up that evening without calling in.

Then, about an hour before closing, Gerald saw Arsen standing by a rack of shoes. He slipped out of the backroom and smiled as he brought a shoebox from beneath the register. The tall man moved gracefully. To Gerald he seemed different than the night before when he appeared gaunt and chalk white. Now his cheeks were flushed as if he had been exposed to a harsh mountain wind.

"Hello, Arsen," Gerald said.

Arsen's eyes narrowed, cut a swathe through Gerald as if he could best be examined in separate pieces. Then his thin lips parted and spread into a warm smile like that between friends seeing each other after being separated for a long time.

"Gerald," he said, placing both porcelain hands on the counter and leaning forward. His breath was mint flavored, although Gerald picked up traces of fresh tilled earth, the effect being like smelling mint leaves stripped from the plant and resting in rich soil.

"Shoes came in today, like I said they would." He came around from behind the counter and handed the box to Arsen. "Let's try them on, see if they fit."

The shoes fit. Arsen walked with ease on the carpeted floor. He swiveled on his feet like Fred Astaire, light and graceful. Gerald commented that he reminded him of the great dancer. Arsen said he appreciated that, he admired the man and had seen all his movies.

"The store is almost empty," Arsen said. His narrow eyes followed Mrs. Warstein as she wandered about, moving behind one display and out another. A young couple walked by carrying bags.

"It's closing time," Gerald said. "But, please, don't hurry. Take your time deciding on the shoes."

"They're fine. I'll take them."

"If there's any problem, anything at all, you bring them back and I'll take care of it."

"You're very passionate about your work," Arsen said. "That's unusual these days."

"I like to make people happy."

Arsen smiled. "We are simple creatures at heart. In such a complicated world. Forgive me, if I am bold," he said. "Are you married, do you have a significant other, as they say?"

Gerald's attempt at a smile turned to a swallow. "No. I live alone." He tried not to look at Arsen's face. "I like living alone. I can do what I want."

"I live alone, too."

"Sometimes it can be scary, living where I do, near the river. You heard about the body they found several miles away, near Cherry Creek?" He almost mentioned the finger but decided against it.

"I heard about it."

"Awful. The poor homeless man." They stood by the register. Arsen paid cash. "I talk to fellows like him all the time when I go to the river. Most of them are good people. Sometimes they help me pick up trash along the riverbank."

"The river can be a dangerous place. Especially at night. Death lurks behind every dark corner."

"There are no corners on a river," Gerald said, "but there are bad places and bad people."

Arsen laughed. "You are a poem, Gerald. There is power in such simplicity and conciseness. I enjoyed this time with you."

Two young women finished their late-night McDonalds hamburgers while they walked on the trail along the South Platte River. They balled up the wrappers and bags and casually tossed them into the woods that bordered the river, laughing. One said it was food for the homeless. The other said they needed to take care of the serial killer terrorizing the city. They stopped when they noticed how quiet the woods had become, and before either could say a word, a shadow enveloped and lifted them both to a high tree limb, breaking their necks in the process. The shadow drained the bodies of fluids, then ripped each one apart piece by piece, painstakingly slow, dropping the body parts along the trunk of the tree.

It planted the legs in the wet muddy bank of the river, pushing the feet in to mid-calf, the result looking like pale shriveled stalks of exotic plants. The shadow impaled the arms on tree limbs. Christmas ornaments. The trunk and head of one woman was tossed into the South Platte to be carried away by the current, until it snagged on a rock or submerged tree. It forced the other woman's head and trunk into a small container on a post by the trail, a container for dog waste. It was a tight fit and the metal bulged almost to bursting, but the shadow made it fit. The body, devoid of liquid, squished into the container the way a tent would be packed in a rucksack.

The shadow rested in the tree, its weight meaningless on the light branches, then retrieved the litter left by the women and disposed of it in the same doggie poo container that held the woman's remains.

It picked out each distinct smell in the area. There were millions. Then it concentrated on distant sounds, since all animal life was silenced in the immediate area. The soft padding of lovers walking on a sidewalk. Someone rustling about in a makeshift tent somewhere up-river. People moving and jostling in their safe beds in nearby apartments. Cars rumbling and exhausting the night air, metal garbage cans in alleyways banging about, the scratch of paper blown along highways, drunks rambling and cursing, and somewhere flesh pounding in a fistfight. The smells and sounds came together all at once, and even with this sensory symphony it still heard thousands of heartbeats and smelled the blood pulsing through miles of arteries and veins.

The shadow floated upwards and blended with the wet laced wind, leaving no trace of its existence save the remains of its dinner.

Arsen visited the store every night that week. He arrived at about the same time, an hour before closing and sat in the same chair. Gerald often sat next to him. Business was slow and Gerald welcomed the company of a man he was intrigued with. He was pleased that Arsen wore the shoes he purchased.

"You don't mind me stopping by, do you?"

"Oh no," Gerald said. "I enjoy hearing about the places where you lived and visited."

Arsen told him about Armenia, Turkey, Greece, Russia, Portugal, Spain, Hungary, Yugoslavia, Germany, and many more. He talked about the beautiful rivers in Europe- the Volga, the Rhine, the Don, Elbe…

"I'm fascinated with rivers – any kind of waterway, really."

Gerald fired off question after question. He couldn't get over how much Arsen had gotten around. "I've never left Denver," Gerald said. Arsen shook his head. "But I read."

He shared with Arsen his love of 19th century literature. He had read *Three Men in a Boat* a dozen times, and Arsen agreed that it was one of his favorite books, too. Gerald had read Thomas Hardy, Mary Shelly, Sir Arthur Conan Doyle, Jules Verne, Bram Stoker, and of course, Edgar Allen Poe. "I know almost everything he has ever written, by heart." He grew silent then, thinking about his friend The Sage, who he hadn't seen for a while.

"You miss your homeless friend," Arsen said, as if he could reach into Gerald's soul.

Gerald's loneliness was spilling out. He wondered if this man next to him could smell loneliness the way he smelled the fragrances of various trees and shrubs and flowers along the riverbank. The way Gerald picked up an earthy and faint decay in Arsen's presence, and the unfamiliar cologne that almost hid the other smells.

One night, Arsen asked Gerald if he had any friends. Gerald said he had many friends, the customers who came in the store, the people he worked with, people he met and talked to on the riverbank. But Gerald knew that Arsen knew the truth. He had few friends.

"I am alone most of the time, too."

Gerald didn't watch television or listen to the radio. He didn't have a computer. His source of news was his co-workers and the people he met near the river. Mrs. Warstein continued to talk about the gruesome murders that held Denver in a state of fear. Police advised everyone to avoid any waterway in the Denver area at night. They beefed up surveillance with men and cameras, but it wasn't enough. The partial remains of two women were just discovered that morning.

Mrs. Warstein, still annoyed with Ted's absence, said, "Don't you hang out at the river every morning and night?" She gave him a teasing, suspicious look. Gerald nodded, thinking what anyone would likely think. It's always the quiet ones.

"You should never venture anywhere near the river when you're alone," she said. "It's too dangerous."

Gerald missed The Sage, and hoped he was all right.

Arsen didn't stop by that night, or the next. Gerald remembered that Arsen enjoyed rivers and creeks as much as he did. "Rivers have always been an important part of my life," Arsen had said several nights ago. "The riverbank is where one can feel large and small at the same time, where one can be strong, or fragile."

Gerald did not understand what he meant by being fragile. He thought of things like fine china, crystal, glass, or plants like dandelions where the softest touch sends the seeds to the wind, or newborn babies and old people. Was that what he meant?

Arsen was old. Gerald worried about him, especially with a maniac on the loose.

Gerald asked Mrs. Warstein if she had seen the old man in the store recently, thinking maybe he had wandered into other departments. Maybe he had tired of Gerald's company.

"What old man?" she asked.

"His name is Arsen. He's been coming here every night just before closing, except for the past few days. You've seen me talking to him."

"I haven't seen any old man. I haven't seen anybody here just before closing. It's been dead around here at night ever since those horrible murders started happening."

"Tall man, distinguished…"

She looked at him like he was crazy. "I'm not in the mood for this," she said, walking away.

She's been under stress, Gerald thought, or maybe she's messing with me.

Arsen. He didn't have any idea where he lived, or what he once did for a living. He knew the geography of Arsen's life, nothing personal except that he shared a love of literature and rivers.

The Sage was gone. Now Arsen.

After work, Gerald went home, changed into his sweat clothes, and walked to the path that led to his favorite spot along the river. It was a chilly night. He didn't see anyone out and about, not even the police, and he assumed people were steering clear of any place close to the river at night.

He sat on a bench between a cluster of cottonwoods. Scraggly brush and a slight muddy grade led to the river. The crescent moon was high over the treetops, dimmed by wispy clouds, and a light wind blew against the left side of his face, carrying with it the fragrances of cottonwood, Indian plum, pine… and a whiff of cologne.

Gerald looked around. It was strangely quiet. He knew wind batted down flying insects, but no birds, no scuttling of nervous animals in the brush and trees, no sounds at all except the rustling branches and leaves and the water rushing nearby.

I shouldn't be here. This is a stupid thing to do. He stood.

Something drifted across the moon. The darkness intensified as if a black net dropped over his body. The smell of cologne and decay. He knew Arsen was nearby.

And far back in his brain he knew he was going to die.

He turned away from the riverbank, and Arsen was there, not more than six feet away. He gasped and fell to one knee. It was too dark to make out any features, but he recognized the cologne and shape of shadow standing there before him, a hastily constructed puzzle of dark menace.

Before he could suck in a breath, he was lifted and placed on the bench. A humming swelled into his ears, and for a long time he drowned in clouds before panic brought him back to the night and soft words. Arsen speaking to him in a slow methodical way, the way a father would speak to a three-year-old son who had just fallen off a swing.

Arsen was beside him. Gerald looked straight ahead at the river, terrified to turn and see what was next to him. They sat that way, in silence, for what seemed an eternity. Eventually, Arsen spoke again.

"I knew you would be here." The water moving swiftly over rocks and against the riverbank accented Arsen's words, a white noise background. "Don't be afraid."

Gerald turned. Arsen, his features blurred and indistinct, yet larger and somehow fierce as if some great predatory beast, the likes he had never seen or read about, was shielded with a giant magnifying glass. Arsen, but not Arsen. It was not human.

The creature opened and closed its mouth exposing jagged teeth. The eyes, mere slits, dull yellow canine eyes that stared straight ahead. It breathed in a slow rhythmic fashion and Gerald found that his breathing was in sync. As the creature's breathing slowed and grew calm, so did Gerald's.

"We are so fragile," Arsen said. "You and me."

"Are you going to kill me?"

"Come. The river." Arsen rose and strayed off the path into patches of weeds and knee-high brush. Gerald followed. They stood on a shelf of rock at the water's edge, listening to the soft rumbling roar of the rapids. Gerald watched the water intently, waiting for an answer.

"Edgar Allen Poe," Arsen said. Then in a gentle voice that barely rose above the sound of the rapids, he recited,

"From childhood's hour I have not been
As others were -- I have not seen
As others saw – I could not bring
My passions from a common spring –
From the same source I have not taken
My sorrow – I could not awaken
My heart to joy at the same tone --'"

Arsen paused and looked at Gerald with a dead calm smile.

Gerald, feeling the creature's stare but keeping his eyes on the moving water, said,

"And all I lov'd – I lov'd alone"

The creature put its arm around him, feather light, and they stared at the water together. "There are bigger rivers," the vampire said. "I would like you to see them."

DISSIDENT

Idea by Jade Kupkim
Story by Max Carrey

The cobblestone streets are plunged in darkness, as the Lamplighter's are paid to keep this section of the city haphazardly lit. I wish I could point a direct finger at who's responsible, but it wouldn't matter because there'd be nothing I could do about it.

I used to be one of the poor, before my Change happened. I remember the filth, the suffocation, and the tears. But I also remember how desperate people can get, ready to stab anyone in the back for a few coins. A thought circles around in my mind: Fathers should protect their daughters…

My head aches and I wince against it.

"What, trudging up old memories?" Steeltooth asks with a laugh, his fangs gleaming metallic in the night.

I shrink away from him, bumping into River, who shoves me off with bloated hands, wafting his signature scent of mildew and algae. I stagger, halting to catch the breath I no longer need.

"We could always pay him a visit," Gob spits, whispering in my ear as his red eyes glow from the shadows.

"You know we're not allowed to touch the Offers," Sagacious murmurs back as he elegantly strides past, trailing the others down a crooked alleyway.

"Offers get paid for their offerings, not much of an offering then is it?" he replies lowly, dribbling saliva. "What a shame we can't touch your old Pops, I'm sure he'd taste as sweet as you did."

Gob disappears into the blackness, and I reluctantly unfurl my fingers from their tightly wound knot.

"I know you're still bitter over what your father did," Leading Light murmurs out of thin air, and I start. His lithe form emerges from the murky fog. "He sold you for money…that must anger you even now."

"Of course it does," I reply truthfully. "He wasn't sure what you'd want me for and he sold me nevertheless."

A gleam of shiny teeth appears in the obscure light.

"Lucky for you we brought you into The Fold… and now you're one of us," Leading Light says as he steps forward, providing me a clear view of his startling features. His heavy black brow and smooth pale skin, with a bottomless ocean for eyes; beautiful yet ugly to me, for I can see what lies beneath. His slender lips form more words, but these he says with an edge. "You might be free from humanistic restraints, but don't think there aren't any rules."

I can feel the slightest breeze hit my cold skin as he walks ahead, throwing a look over his shoulder back to me.

"Come, Delicate," he orders.

"Emma," I spitefully whisper, and I can see his muscles tense, though he refuses to acknowledge he heard me. "Emma…"

Pitifully, I dutifully follow.

The alley bends into differing directions as the hodgepodge of buildings jut out at odd angles. Yet we, The Fold, travel with light feet, barely stirring the puddles, slicing dexterously through the air.

Coming upon the scent of a human their jaws snap and their tongues lick eager lips. My heart swells with the longing to satiate my thirst. My throat yearns for that thick metallic warmth to run down and fill me up. I can practically smell the blood…her blood.

A ragged middle aged woman with a devious glint in her eye flits about nervously on her toes before us.

"My, my," Steeltooth moans, as he leans in and takes a big sniff of her.

The woman shivers.

Gob smacks his lips, River stretches his face into a puffy smile, while Sagacious poses in a corner, stoically restricting himself from lurching forward and tearing out her throat.

I don't trust myself. I can feel my fingernails itch to sink into her flesh, so I keep behind Leading Light, letting him block as much of her scent and pulsing veins from me as his figure can.

"You have all that you've promised?" Leading Light asks with a tone of greedy anticipation.

"Yes, exactly as I offered," the Offer concurs. "I'll take you."

"What are we getting this time?" Gob asks Leading Light as we follow the Offer into a back entrance of a rundown building.

Moonlight cascades through patches of exposed roofing, shedding light on rats that skitter away into darkened rooms.

"You'll see, just a moment longer," Leading Light replies, the smile returning to his lips.

I know the question is more *who* than *what*. I admit I don't always dislike the sensation of killing, when it's someone that has it coming, but the helpless make my stomach churn. That's why I'm called Delicate.

Peeling wallpaper of what once used to be a well adorned house surrounds us, fragments of a life now gone, as poor side turns to poorer side.

The floorboards are bloated from rainwater and overflowing sewage from the lavatory pipes. I pinch my nose against the putrid smell, making a strong effort to appear to be bothered by it so the others don't tease and torment me, because it's really my thirst that has begun to overwhelm me.

The Offer had smelled tantalizing at first, but the longer I taste the air around her the more she reeks of muck, as if tar runs through her veins. So why has my hunger bloomed, am I really that desperate? No… there's something sweet cutting through the sludge.

Steeltooth and Sagacious stop, their eyes going wide with bloodlust.

"You smell that?" Steeltooth murmurs. "Humans…"

"Not just any humans," Sagacious says, throwing a look of voracious surprise to Leading Light.

They both set off in a dash, following the scent rather than the Offer. River trails behind, and Gob thunders after them. I still keep behind Leading Light, who walks coolly through a trashed living room. Cockroaches scurry away from us, and we turn a corner into a hallway.

The glowing white light of the moon flickers at the end of the hall where the kitchen resides. My ears pick up several muffled cries that cause my breath to catch in my throat. No wonder my thirst is so strong. A waft of sweet pumping blood coats my nostrils confirming my fears…children.

I bulldoze past Leading Light, skidding to a halt upon the kitchen tiles. Children are bound and gagged, tears streaking down their red blotchy faces, succulent faces… I shake my head to rid the thought, though my mouth waters.

Leading Light laughs as he enters the room with the Offer. His expression is nastily glorious, feasting in the image of the twelve bound children, sniveling on the floor with their backs pressed against each other.

Steeltooth is flicking his fingers against one of the children's heads, giggling. Sagacious is leaned up against the wall eying a pair of twins in matching braids. River and Gob dance around the space, before Gob stoops low to lick a child's face, causing the poor boy to tremble.

My nerves are alight with fire and every inch of my being begs to join them, yet their plump little faces all soured in crying cause my eyes to flex as if they would tear if they could.

"Twelve orphans, just as I promised," the Offer exclaims, holding out her palm.

Leading Light pulls a hefty bag from his pocket, dropping it in her hand, and the coins inside chink against each other.

"You're invited to watch if you wish," Leading Light tells the woman proudly as she spills the coins out, counting them with eager eyes.

"No thank you kind Sir," she replies, stuffing her earnings away. "It seems I've got some money to spend."

She bends low to the smallest child, no older than four, and pats him on the head. He looks up to her with desperate eyes shimmering with tears.

"Tata little one, now be a good boy and be a tasty treat," she cackles, her voice shaking the rickety foundation as she slinks away.

I growl after her, wishing I could tear her limb from limb, but instead I turn my wrath to Leading Light and murmur viciously, "You've done this to test me, haven't you?"

I catch a glint in his evil blue eyes, then suddenly his arms outstretch like Jesus speaking to his disciples. "Tonight we feast!"

Gob lunges.

"No!" I yell, dashing forward, but I'm too late.

Gob has already sunk his teeth into a boy. The child twitches and spasms against him, blood running down his throat.

My nails claw Gob's face. His red eyes flare in fury as he cries out, gurgling blood. But Sagacious throws himself at me, I smash into the floor, causing the tile to crack and snap around me. Drawing up my knee I kick Sagacious in the chest. He stumbles back, lips curled into a snarl, teeth chomping for my flesh.

Steeltooth yanks me back by my arm just as I grab a fistful of Gob's shirt, and we both are hurled against the far wall, plummeting with a thud.

River claps his hands and laughs as the children's stifled screams echo against my eardrums. The dead boy suspended by his bonds burns in my wavering vision.

Gob whimpers next to me, scuttling forward as he licks his bloody fingers, heading for more of his victim, the thirst overtaking him. I grab him by the nape of his neck and go to yank him back, but Sagacious barrels forward and digs his claws into me.

My spine is ground into the wall, and I let out a scream as it crumbles beneath me, pieces of plaster breaking away. The pain dies quickly, the benefit of being a vampire, and I surge through, pitching myself forward.

I bite off the tip of Sagacious' nose and spit it back at him. He yelps, falling backward, as his hands swat at his face in surprise.

Steeltooth slams me backward just as I try to peel myself from the wall. His fingers claw my head back, splaying my neck vulnerable before him. I can feel his metallic fang graze my throat just as Leading Light yells.

"Stop!"

Sagacious calms his steaming hatred, River stays his hands, Gob sits eyeing his kill hungrily, and Steeltooth growls before pulling away from me.

"I warned you…there are rules," Leading Light says as he kneels down in front of me. Though his tone is disappointed, his eyes seem to shine with entertainment. He was expecting me to act like this, this is fun to him.

Twisting up my face, I sneer as I spit, "This is wrong! We might be predators, but there's no hunt in this…no purpose of this!"

"You would save the innocent little brats?" he chuckles. "Their full potential is filling our stomachs… No one tastes sweeter than a child. Well," an eyebrow arches, "babies do, but I wanted enough for us to share."

"You sicken me."

"As do you, Delicate…stop fighting what you are."

"Only when it stops conflicting with *who* I am."

A grin screws up the side of his mouth into a smug expression. He runs a hand through his glossy hair as he stands back up. Staring down at me, before looking to his followers, he proclaims, "Two for each of you, and we'll see if she comes to her senses once the feast really begins. If not, we'll quarter up the rest and deal with her later."

The children's sobs continue to ring out against the stale air. Their feet kick, and their little hands tug at the ropes uselessly. Five burly but inhumanly lithe forms poised to strike are preparing to feast, but six pairs of fangs glisten in the night… with one emerging from the shadows.

A floorboard creaks, causing all of us to start and whip our heads toward it. The Stranger is cloaked in black robes. His skin isn't pale but russet in color, and his eyes burn with flames. He's like us, but also different, better, for there is an air about him that is undeniable.

"What is this?" he asks with a deep growl as he enters the room, "What have you done?"

He's only heard when he wants to be heard, only seen when he wants to be seen. I couldn't even smell his fragrant sulfur musk until he allowed it. I know, because I can see the way he commands attention. Leading Light is bowing before him. Gob stumbles back and the others fall into line. Even I push myself up to stand, but refuse to go near the others. I want his impression of me to be unassociated with them. He's so beautiful and raw with dominion, unlike the masquerading brutes of our Fold.

"Master, are you not pleased?" Leading Light whines in a shivering tone. "I would have my men feast upon the sweetest blood, for then we shall be invigorated, satiated beyond simple need and able to do your work at our utmost."

The Stranger's facial muscles twitch in ire, his eyes burning a crackling violent flame. His voice booms, "This is frivolous! You do not do this for me, for if you did you would replenish on aged blood and save the young for greater purposes."

"But-"

"Silence! You fool… you would grant yourself a more supple meal than see the advantage these children offer…" The Stranger pauses to glance upon me.

My knees droop, and I fight the urge to curl inward on myself, as his gaze is so strong and haunting. But suddenly, The Stranger's face softens. It envelops me in warmth, a rarity, something I only now find in blood. The heat feels good, rousing something to life inside of me.

Yet his face hardens again as he turns back to Leading Light, finishing, "…if you reared them."

Leading Light fumbles backward, catching himself on the counter. The light from the windows cut streaks across his bewildered face.

"You would have us raise children?"

"Train up a child in the way he should go, and when he is old, he will not depart from it," The Stranger says with a firm voice.

My dead heart swells. My smile awakens for the children, for they are safe in the arms of The Stranger.

"These children are not food," The Stranger continues, "they are warriors to be trained, to be gifted and be greater than the generation before them!"

Leading Light and the others look on furiously. Gob and River direct their hatred toward the children, staring at them as if they wish to squash them under their boot heels, while Steeltooth and Sagacious clench their jaws and stare defiantly at The Stranger.

"You were blind to see their potential, yet she…" The Stranger motions toward me, raising a russet hand with charcoaled nails, his black squared pupils locking onto me, "she saw their worth."

My smile deepens with the passionate longing of desire. Desire to be in his favor, in his grace, by his side… it tugs at me with deep rooted instinct.

Leading Light throws a twisted snarl my way, saying, “Delicate is weak and-”

“You refuse to listen and continue to speak your drivel,” The Stranger interjects, voice raised, teeth bared. “For a final time I tell you, silence… I am disappointed in you Leading Light, and as such I revoke your title.”

Leading Light clenches his hands into fists. His eyes turn furious, and he growls, flashing his fangs. His lips part, an unneeded breath sucks in through his teeth, and he screams, “I am Leading Light, leader of-”

“I told you, silence!” The Stranger roars so loudly it deafens all other sounds. In less than a single moment, with nails stuck out like razor blades he slices them across Leading Light’s neck.

Blood sprays the ceiling, drips off The Stranger’s charcoaled nails, staining them red. Leading Light’s head twists round his neck, a screwed up expression of anger, shock and pain frozen on his face. Then his head lobs off, falling from his shoulders, and rolls across the tile until coming to a stop at my feet.

The Stranger’s eyes are emblazed so strongly I can feel the heat of their flames pulsating off them, yet a satisfied smile stretches across his face.

Gob snivels, River hides his face in his hands, while Steeltooth and Sagacious are paralyzed with limbs limp and eyes wide. The children hide their heads, but some that have watched seem almost pleased, and why shouldn't they? He was going to eat them.

Sound returns to me. I can listen to the wonderful scrape of Leading Light's teeth against the floor as I shove his head away with a kick. Turning my gaze to the cleanly sliced muscle and tissue of his neck, I know there's no way he's coming back from this. He's dead for good, and good riddance to him. He took everything from me, and he's gotten exactly what he deserved.

A devious smile creeps up my face.

"Do any of you wish to contend with me?" The Stranger asks, stepping forward to the others who shrink away from him in fear, shaking their heads. "No? Good…You," he points to Gob, "for your dissidence you shall deal with Leading Light's body and the child you murdered."

Gob fumbles over his words, a clang of jumbled up mess, but I can just make out, "Yes Master," as he pathetically begins scooping up the bodies with trembling hands.

The sting of sulfur hits my nostrils, and I look up to see The Stranger before me. The fire in his eyes have calmed, and his demeanor is pleasant, soothing even. He stretches out a russet hand, saying, "You, my child, are not Delicate…I would grant you control of this Fold, if you would have it, and I shall call you Luminary."

The others whip their heads around, shock etched upon their features. Leading Light's head falls from Gob's hands with a thump, until he collects himself and bustles to grab it again.

I reach out my hand, but hesitate a moment. My palm hovers above his.

"Raise our children to shine," he tells me. "Teach them the way of the vampire, and they will want for nothing. Amass sheep for the Shepherd?"

I don't want the children to die, but… they're not going to stay that way. What he's offering is the best of both worlds, and he's giving me the opportunity to do right by them. Unlike what Leading Light did to me, what my father did, what this unholy government has done.

I can raise an army of justice, to take on those that would unlawfully punish. Rid the leaders of London that would see these people in squalor, those that would backstab their fellow brethren, and even hold the members of The Fold accountable.

I drop my hand into his and a connection sparks between our flesh. In so doing I pledge myself to him, to serve under him, as my one true Master.

His name rings clear in my head without needing to be spoken. He's the master of flame, the master of Hell. The Devil.

"Come Luminary, lead your Fold," he instructs me.

As soon as I blink The Devil is gone, taking his sweet smelling sulfur, his kind violent eyes, and his smooth russet skin with him. I wish he was still here, for the room feels sickened without his presence. But he's left me with excitement tingling in my veins as I feel the light to lead stir within me.

I'm no longer Emma. I was never Delicate. I'm Luminary.

"Release the children," I order Steeltooth, then to Sagacious, "You too."

They look between each other for a moment, their jaws flexing and their teeth gnawing at their cheeks, but Sagacious' wisdom rouses and he nods to me, loosening his tensed muscles. Steeltooth follows suit, though with a look of repugnance.

Gob is still cleaning, and River begins to regain his confidence, staring at me studiously.

They will learn to respect me, to love me, and if not they will be given what they are due.

The first child whose bonds fall gives her leave to dash for freedom, but I grab her frail little arm. She struggles against me, but I hold her still. Kneeling down, wafting her tender scent, ignoring the urge of thirst, I tell her, "Don't worry…it'll only hurt for a moment."

SPLINTERS

by

Keawe Melina Patrick

The man came into my life at the Home Depot. He meandered along the aisle as I mumbled, "Can't pass this up."

Tall and brawny, he stared over my shoulder. "Pass what up?"

With a blister-packed flashlight in each palm, I pointed at a display arrayed from small to large. "Look, the mini-flash is 50 bucks, the medium $12.95, and the mega $100."

"Something's priced wrong."

"Yes, sir."

"Going to tell the manager?"

"Yep."

"Better get one then." He grinned.

His teeth resembled a saber-toothed cat's.

"Those are some caps."

He tapped a tooth. "Aren't they?"

We went separate ways, and I doubted we'd meet again. I never imagined that because of him, I'd become a murderer.

But a week later, at the Romping Gator, while the Ravens trounced the Packers, a shadow fell over my pale ale. I glanced up.

A neon yellow glow washed over him as his lips twitched with a hint of mischief.

He gestured to the empty seat beside me. “Who’s winning?”

I nodded for him to sit. “Ravens.”

He extended a hand. “Jackson Leonard.”

Loud music played, and I shook my head as I offered my hand. “Leopard?”

“Leonard!” He yelled.

“Scott Revell.”

Leonard waggled a finger at the bartender and ordered a Tequila Sunrise.

I returned my attention to the game and flipped one of the bar’s advertising pencils through my fingers. I’d memorized the stamped-on slogan years ago: The *Romping Gator, Hottest Gator Balls, this side of Hell. We Deliver.*

In silence, Leonard and I watched the screen until the bottom of my mug dried, and he pulled it toward his. “Another?”

“No, thanks.”

“You can’t be a lightweight.”

Last March, I’d finished my 20 in the marines and continued the training regime. “Not much of a drinker.” I hooked a thumb at the TV. “You play?”

He slid his glass in figure eights through condensation on the bar-top. “Not since college.” A crooked grin revealed those fangs. “Good times.”

At Home Depot, his canine hadn't been cracked. Open-mouthed, I tongued mine. "How'd you get the chip?"

"Same way everybody breaks teeth, eating something I shouldn't."

He leaned over and sniffed me. I jumped, tipping the stool. "Mister, you're not my type."

People stopped talking and stared.

He laughed. "Whoa, a misunderstanding."

I slapped a 20 down. "Yeah, right."

For a few seconds, I faced him before heading to the door. Outside, I strode to the unlit overflow lot. Not even the crickets chirped. The guy got my hackles up, that's all. I shook it off and tromped over the rocks to my pickup. Beeped the locks open, slid in, and put the key in the ignition by feel. All while I scanned the darkness.

I clicked the headlights on. Leonard stood, arms crossed, six feet in front of the hood. Those fangs on full display.

"What the fuck?" I peeled out and sprayed half a dozen cars with gravel.

Three weeks passed, and the mild spring morphed into a balmy summer. By June 27th, I'd almost forgotten Leonard.

As Sarah and I strolled along the boardwalk, he popped up again.

"Hey there, Scott." He wore cutoff jeans and a Hawaiian shirt.

We stopped because he blocked the sidewalk. I bobbed a finger as if thinking. "Jackson, isn't it?"

"That's right. How've you been, and who's this ravishing lady?"

Minus Sarah, I'd have stepped around. But her brows lifted in that, *I'm curious*, tilt. "Sarah Sandor, meet Jackson Leopard."

"Leonard."

I knew his damn name.

He clasped her hands. "Delighted, Miss."

When he didn't let go, she pulled free. "Sarah."

"Thank you." Jackson squinted at me. "Mind if I join you?"

Hell yes. "No, but we're on our way home."

"So am I."

Sarah made small talk and seemed charmed by Leonard. I walked behind, fists at my side. The only player in on Leonard's game was Leonard.

At the Ford, Sarah touched the door. "This is ours."

Leonard pointed over a block. "I'm there."

Not for a hummingbird's heartbeat did I believe he parked anywhere in the vicinity. Eyes narrowed, I tipped my chin toward the pickup bed. "Want a ride?"

A window-rattling laugh echoed off the buildings. "Worried about me, Scott? Somebody gonna attack a seven-foot guy?"

I opened Sarah's door, and she slid in. Then rounded the hood and climbed in without another word—my eyes on him.

Outside Sarah's house, we kissed. Deep, warm, and sweet. The temptation to take it inside grew in our body tension and lingering caresses. We'd spent nights together before, but we both worked early Friday morning. She tugged on my hand, and

I almost stayed anyway. But her prune-lipped neighbors came out on their porch glaring. A last kiss, and we made a dress-up date for Saturday evening at her favorite restaurant.

Friday night, I watched *The Dirty Dozen* yet again and ate takeout salad in the living room.

Someone pounded on my front door. I almost slopped blue cheese down my shirt. When I opened the screen, two men stared at me.

"Are you Scott Revell?"

I nodded and swallowed a bite of chicken.

The tall man removed his hat and gestured past me toward the living room. "I'm Detective Conway. This is Officer Donovan. Mind if we come in?"

"Sure." I shrugged. Confused, I sat on the edge of my recliner next to the bowl of wilting lettuce. Conway took a seat on the couch nearest me, and Donovan hiked his equipment belt before wedging into an armchair.

I rubbed my scruffy chin. "What's this about?"

Conway placed the hat beside him. "According to Mr. and Mrs. Jerome Sandor, you were dating their daughter, Sarah."

My heart pounded at the *were dating*. "Yes, *I am.* Aren't Jerome and Betty on a cruise in Egypt?"

"Yes, they're on the Nile trying to charter a flight to the States." He licked his lips. "I'm sorry to inform you of Sarah Sandor's death."

"That's impossible."

"I know this is a lot to take in, but with the Sandors unavailable, we want you to accompany us to the morgue."

"Sarah's parents would've called me."

"They don't have cell coverage. The local authorities tracked them down for us."

For a few moments, the men faded into the background. My vision tunneled to a black velvet box on my fireplace mantle. Blood swooshed through my ears as my eyes jerked from the engagement ring to Sarah's picture next to it.

"Mr. Revell? Donovan, get him some water."

I held up a hand. "No." My voice cracked, and I couldn't breathe. "But, you're wrong."

"Identification is purely procedural."

Saliva flooded my mouth, and my gut clenched. I swallowed. "I'll get my wallet and keys."

Donovan glanced down. "And shoes."

"Uh, yeah." Each step leaden, I turned back to them. "What happened?"

Conway crossed his arms. "Not sure yet. Her throat's ripped out."

As soon as I entered the morgue, formaldehyde fumes stung my sinuses. Farther into the over-bright room, Sarah lay on a stainless-steel table with a sheet pulled up to her shoulders. The cloth failed to cover the wound.

I scrubbed a hand over my face. Tried to erase the image in front of me. Tried not to gape at a cavity the size of my fist above her collar bone.

Delicate tendons and bones protruded from a spot I'd kissed thousands of times. My abs rippled as anger built inside me.

A tear splashed on her face. The officer stepped close but was too slow to stop me. I brushed my thumb over her moist cheek and kissed her lips. No longer supple, no longer responsive, no longer Sarah.

The coppery tang of blood defiled her lilac perfume. It wasn't until I straightened that I spotted the bite on her opposite jugular—two precise punctures.

"Jesus Christ!" I snarled at the officer. "Do you have the bastard?"

"No, sir, not yet."

I clamped my jaw so hard the muscles ached.

"Any idea who would do this to Miss Sandor?"

I paused before meeting his eyes. "No."

That afternoon, I stopped by an ex-marine buddy's shady pawnshop. When we shook goodbye, I wore an untraceable .45 revolver in a shoulder holster. I didn't want to shoot Leonard. Just manipulate him to a place where I could wrap my arm around his neck and choke the living shit out of him.

By evening, I sat at my usual stool at the Gator. Settled in, not even pretending to glance at the big screen. I bird-dogged the door. Let the ale go flat. Fiddled with a pencil. He'd show. All I have left is endless time.

As dawn broke Monday, I picked up Sarah's parents from the airport. The rest of the morning, we planned her funeral. Tuesday afternoon, I stood next to her dad at the visitation. It was tough helping two of the nicest people I'd ever met cope with the loss of their only child. Numbness set in while I stared at the overly made-up, rigid body of the woman I loved.

Later, Leonard walked into the bar, beaming as if he'd won the lottery. He strode past me and directly out the back door. I pursued him into the lot, but he was nowhere in sight. I screamed his name, but only the night breeze whispered back to me.

On the Fourth of July, a week after Sarah and I laughed on the promenade and fed each other fried clam strips, her parents and I buried her.

Walking inside the Gator that evening, my dress shoes stuck for a second to someone's spilled beer. After this thing with Leonard was settled, I'd never come back. I unbuttoned my black suit jacket and reluctantly asked for Sarah's favorite—a margarita. In my left hand, I held a red rose from the splay on her coffin. I tucked the flower into my lapel and plucked another oversized pencil from the enamel cup. I probably had more of these than the bar did. For a while, I limbered my fingers, got bored, and slipped it into a side pocket.

"Heard about Sarah." Leonard patted my back.

My muscles bunched, oh, how I wanted to break each of his knuckles. Instead, my fingernails squeaked as they dug into the vinyl seat cover.

"Sorry for your loss, Scott. Sarah was extraordinary."

Rage dumped adrenaline into me, but I kept my voice steady. "Thanks."

"Let's blow this place. I've got a bottle of Macallan single malt made for a melancholy night."

"Yeah, sure."

Out front, Leonard climbed into a black Porsche Cayenne parked in a handicapped spot.

"Didn't realize you were disabled, Jackson."

He laughed. "Only to the extent that I never take an extra step I don't have to."

We pulled into the street and headed north. I swiveled into a position better for removing the .45.

A misty rain fell, and he clicked on the wipers. "Do I smell gun oil?"

I lifted the weapon from the shoulder holster and sniffed it before aiming at him. "You have a hell of a nose."

"Yes, I do. And do you know my favorite scent in the entire world?"

I remained motionless.

"Lilac."

My finger twitched on the trigger, but crowded sidewalks stopped me.

"I detected Sarah's perfume at the hardware store, combined with her own sweet fragrance." He pulled over into an empty park and cut the ignition. "I followed you until you led me to her.

Then I watched the two of you for a while. You were—cute—together." Leonard sighed. "A shame we'll not make it to my house. The Macallan's excellent."

I moved the trigger a hairsbreadth, but I eased the pressure off. For a moment, we sat in silence. Cars passed, illuminating the Porsche, silhouettes of us elongating, then fading.

I waved the gun at his face. "What's with the veneers?"

"You think I have dentures?"

"Whatever. Those blades in your mouth butchered Sarah's neck. And you may as well have signed the right side."

"God, you're dense. I thought you'd figured it out."

"What?"

"I'm not human." He laughed and stroked the barrel of the gun. "Bullets can't kill me. They'll make a mess of my suit though, which I always resent. Fittings are a pain in the ass."

"You're worried about the suit?"

"And I enjoy driving this car. Hate to get rid of it."

A purple mini with blue LED underbody lights parked nearby. And a teenage couple emerged with a six-pack, perched on the hood, and drank. The car illuminated the tree line and created a glow inside the Cayenne.

Leonard's voice had mesmerized me, but the car pulling in broke the effect. I shifted and brought the gun closer to him in an awkward face off. "Why did you kill her?"

He extended a palm, then closed his fist as if catching a lightning bug. “Sarah’s scent delighted me, and I hungered.”

I gouged the end of the barrel into his chest. His eyes met mine as I pulled the trigger. With each squeeze, it dug deeper. On the revolver’s sixth shot, my knuckles pressed against his ribs.

He snatched the gun, dislocating my index finger with a snap. “Look at my suit.”

“You’re not dead.”

Still bending my wrist with his free hand, he brushed the ragged fabric of his shirt. “This was Italian. Idiot.”

The mini’s motor roared, its tires squealing.

An instant later, his hands crushed me to the passenger door. “Thanks to you, asshole, I have to hunt and kill those kids in that ridiculous car. And I’m not even hungry.”

I gasped, “What are you?”

“A vampire.”

He pressed me harder into the door, and my left arm snapped below the elbow. The pencil in my right pocket stabbed through the fabric into my wrist. Blood oozed around my watch band. A second shove and Sarah’s funeral rose squished into my face. Its stale odor elicited a hazy image of her body. “No!” I raised my leg and kicked him in the gut. A move as effective as punting a refrigerator.

He nipped my neck. “AB negative and drug-free. What a treat.”

The pain became inconsequential as the magnitude of my inadequacies tallied in my head.

Failure to protect Sarah. Failure to revenge her murder. Failure to survive.

He released me.

"You'll die, but not soon." The engine purred. "I'm taking you home to savor." He shifted into reverse and turned the wheel.

I growled, pulled the wood through my flesh with my teeth, and spat it into my hand. My crushed left arm snagged on the console as I lunged sideways, aiming for Leonard's heart. The pencil stabbed deep into his bicep.

Leonard's face reflected the orange dashboard lights. "Revell, you son of a bitch!"

He backhanded me. The blow threw me sideways and shattered my jaw.

The SUV coasted backward, bumped a tree, and stalled.

"Well, Scott, this is inconvenient." When he touched the wood, his fingertips sizzled and burned onto the surface. Under the charring skin, embers sparkled and glowed. It resembled fire spreading in a high wind. A fetid haze filled the Porsche, redolent of singed hair. The shimmer spread up his neck with a soft fizz.

I jerked the door handle, but the safety locks kept me inside.

"Scott." He whispered.

I turned toward him.

He sat still, his clothes incinerated, skin burnished to a glossy flint. "Sarah was ambrosial. I shared her with my friends." After a few seconds, he twisted toward me. As he turned, flakes of his face sheared like glacial ice falling into the sea. His words slurred, "She was orgasmic."

I breathed in a ragged gulp and punched him. Ash swirled in a choking cloud.

The next blow crumbled him into a pile of coarse soot.

I crawled over Leonard's cremains. My palm landed on the Gator pencil, and I took it. Both arms broken, I fumbled the door open and sucked cold air before staggering into the night. Down the road, a gas station shined like the Holy Grail. I crossed my arms tight to my chest and walked. Behind me, the Cayenne exploded.

For over ten years, I've peered side-eyed at people's teeth as if an undercover dentist. All this time, I thought, an eon-old species couldn't even survive a damn splinter. Always careful, I kept a sharpened Gator pencil with me.

At first, the nip bothered me. When nothing happened, though, I figured I'd watched too many horror movies. I mean, Leonard only tasted me. Sometimes, I'd rub the tiny scars. Still, the vampire thing became dreamlike, leaving me mourning Sarah's loss.

The day before yesterday, I accidentally jabbed my hand with a Gator as I emptied my pockets. The tip's bare wood penetrated kind of deep, but when I pulled it out, no blood wept from the injury. This morning, the center where the lead hit was a healthy pink, and so was the surrounding skin. It left a black donut of ash. I dug it out with my knife, and the donut filled in healthy. I was wrong about the splinters.

Then I had lunch with my brother and bit my lip. I dashed into the men's room and checked the mirror. My canines had grown.

I've never been suicidal, but I'll keep a Gator on me. For now, I need to figure out how much wood those monsters—we monsters—can tolerate. Maybe it varies.

If the impulse to kill came, I wouldn't murder someone else's Sarah.

I sure have missed Sarah's lilac perfume, though. At dinner, a girl, four tables away, wore the same enticing scent. It floated in the air like a path right to her.

INVADERS IN WALLACHIA

by

Luke Frostick

Your eminence, these papers were discovered at the burned out camp of the Sultan before the walls of Târgovişte. It is the account of an infidel outrider whose name is not recorded here. It covers events in Wallachia in the year of our lord 1462. I trust that your eminence will quickly see why it should not be disseminated even within our brotherhood. I send it to your eminence to dispose of or keep for the records as you see fit.

Your servant: István.

Spring 866

The sultan gathered his army outside Constantinople: Proud Sipahis, disciplined janissaries, colourful Aḳıncı with their waxed moustache and the Topçu Ocağı standing by their guns. Above us all the Sanjaks of the Pashas fluttered in glorious shades of green and red. At our head, sultan Mehmet rode with the Kapıkulu Süvarileri around him and his Silahdars awaiting his commands. We performed the namaz as one before the walls of the city, the very same walls that Mehmet, our sultan, had breached not ten years prior.

With the flags flying we marched. The mehter bölüğü led the way, their horns screeching and the great drums shaking the earth, driving the djinn out of their holes and frightening them out of our the Sultan's path. The House of Osman was going to war again.

The prince of Wallachia, in his arrogance, had forgotten to whom he owed his throne, declined to pay his tithes to the Porte and even gone so far as to raid south of the Danube, slaughtering Muslims who lived there and violating their bodies on stakes. He would know that the Sultan's vengeance was upon him. He would know it by the sound of those drums.

As we marched north past Edirne, our numbers were swelled by Christian knights, vassals of the Sultan and more Aḳıncı bringing the army to the largest number seen since the fall of Constantinople.

The enemy made an attempt to stop us at the Danube, contesting us in the river and firing arrows as we crossed, but the Sultan's army could not be resisted by such an insignificant force and they were made to withdraw.

The Prince of Wallachia could not join us in open battle, but instead chose to harass our army with horsemen, archers and local bandits. The Sultan, to counter this threat, dispatched bands of Aḳıncı, lightly armoured riders to raid the countryside and counter the prince's bandit tactics. Seeking bounty and glory for myself, I attached myself to Yusuf Ağa's Aḳıncı band. With his wolf skin cloak, waxed mustache and wide starring eyes, Yusuf Ağa had been fighting across Anatolia and the Balkans his entire life. He could keep even the wildest rider under firm control.

We struck north west to harry the enemy where we could, live off the land, track the Prince's main army and keep an ever watchful eye for Hungarians. If Matthias Corvinus was to come to his fellow Christian's aid, our Sultan would need to know as soon as humanly possible.

The going was rough, the landscape was steep and covered in dense blankets of grim pines. The first few nights we slept rough, up against our horses. The villages, hamlets and hovels we'd hope to raid were desperately poor. Only the old watched us, eyes dead to our passing, to the filthy children screaming in the dirt of the hunger that hollowed them out. Any hopes of plunder were swiftly dashed. Even the prospect of living off the land seem hollow. The Prince in his retreat had scorched the earth, salted the fields and carried away anything of use or value along with his army, leaving the serfs to starve. On occasion we ran into Wallachian scouts and their own raiders. They fought bravely and refused to retreat or yield but, with thanks to Allah, could not outride or outfight us. We soon found why they fought with such vigour. The roads were lined with corpses run through on wooden stakes and left for the birds, captured brother Muslims and plenty of Christians. Yusuf Ağa told us that the Prince had no qualms with killing those suspected of cowardice or disloyalty in his uniquely brutal style.

On the third day of the campaign, we spotted a village that seemed to be in better shape than the others we had passed. Unwilling to pass by on our first chance of profit, we rode down swords and bows at the ready.

This village, though larger than those we had previously encountered was still in dire poverty. The son of the Dragon, Prince of Wallachia was nothing if not thorough and efficient. The mill was empty, the animals driven off or killed and only a few of the old and very young peasants left behind to survive as best they could. Of course there were also the stakes laid out to greet us.

We stopped to water our horses so we could move on again with haste.

"You'll not want to be doing that." A voice said. A woman as worn and bent as a great olive tree hailed us. She spoke Turkish to us, not unheard of amongst the Bulgars, Saxons and Romans, but unexpected enough for us to turn our heads.

"Why is that grandmother?"

"The Prince's men, they poisoned the well. The Prince's dogs think that murdering our village would be a fair price to kill one of you or maybe just a horse or two."

"*Jazaka Allahu Khairan,*" I said thanking her. "You are the first person who's been willing to talk to us, let alone help us."

"Bhaa, what do I owe that Prince? I thought by doing you a good turn you would spare our village the fire as well. We've not got much left except shelter."

"We would have fed ourselves and moved on." That was not the truth. "But I see now that you don't have any for us to take."

"The old men have been able to pull a fish or two out of the river and the children have been trying their luck catching sparrows, but what kind of meal is that? It has been said that you Turks would burn every village to the ground in your war."

"This is a just war, the Prince is a usurper, who has done much evil to his neighbours. My Sultan's aim is simply to place the Impaler's brother Radu Bey on the throne. With help from God, he will rule with more wisdom."

The old woman didn't seem convinced by my justification. She sucked he gums thinking, a caterpillar of a scowl on her brow. "They are all cut from the same cloth, both sons of the dragon. I don't see how a pet dragon is less dangerous than a wild one. That Prince, Vlad, when he feuded with the Transylvanian saxons, he impaled any that he could get his hands on. Once, he saw that there was a great number of beggars on the streets of Târgoviște. He tricked them into a building then burned them alive. Afterwards, he claimed to be the first monarch to have solved poverty." The old woman seemed more angry about the lie than the killing. "That kind of madness and evil is not limited to one man, oh no. Nothing good can come out of that house, it would perhaps be better if god whipped them all of the face of the earth."

"I can not agree with you Grandmother. Radu Bey is a good Muslim and a good man, god willing he will be a prince who rules justly. Even now I know he is riding out in the land, getting supporters to his side and fighting the against The Impaler." She was unconvinced and her expression reminded me of a cat, lifted from its resting place and put upon another cushion.

"You have it all mixed up my son." She said. "Good Christian, good Muslim, all words to cover up the truth. They are strong that is all that matters. You will have to be too my dear Muslim knight or you will be like us waiting for death here. We will last till the winter, then the fish will go and the small birds will hide. We will strip the trees, boil the bark to put something into us, then we will die. Hopefully God will spare us from turning on each other. Truth be told, Turk, I was hoping you would be the savage infidels I've heard of from other campaigns, who would cut our heads off and be done with it."

I told her to not fear, that the Sultan would be victorious and there would be supplies for all once the fighting was done. I told her that Radu Bey was, though now a Muslim, of her race that he would take care of them. She remained unimpressed.

Yusuf Ağa judged the hills to be clear and the enemy to be many miles away decided to stay in the village for the night. A decision that was most welcome for me. We at small amounts of bread and olives and occupied a barn for ourselves and our horses. We set up a watch and bedded down the nostalgic scent of the horses.

Yusuf Ağa was to take the first watch himself and I was to relieve him before the Tahajjud, but I found it difficult to sleep. My conversation with the old woman rattled round my brain like a stone in my shoe, making it impossible to get comfortable, so I got up to relieve my captain early.

I didn't find him at his post. That was troubling. Yusuf Ağa was a veteran raider who knew the importance of the watch. Also, there was something about the quality of the night. It was crisp, cold, oppressed by a silence that rolled out of the hills, making me reach down for the comforting pommel of my sword.

"Yusuf Ağa?" I asked, the uncanny left me with little hope that he'd simply gone to relieve himself, that same feeling did not let me belt out his name at the top of my lungs.

I heard a snap. That sound could only been one thing; it doesn't change from a chicken wing to a horse's knee. Bones being pulled apart and the tendons between them popping sounds the same in all God's creatures. It just gets louder in bigger beasts. Another one followed just as grizzly. My unwilling eyes followed the sound to its source, one of the hovels, a pile of unpointed stone with a mushy thatch roof.

The doorway and crumbling lintel beckoned me in, what little light the moon shone on that hut was snuffed out after it crossed the threshold. I heard the sound of liquid slap down onto the stone like a maid had thrown down her washcloth in frustration. I walked towards it. My body told me to run, my intellect offered the same advice and my soul dreaded what I might find through that door, but I was an Aḳıncı, my honour drove me forward while everything that was bestial in me begged me to run.

I put my foot across the threshold. The room smelled of iron, blood and dirt. Suspended in the air was Yusuf Ağa. Blood ran down his arm, hung on his finger tips and plopped onto the dirt floor. It leaked from the boney stump that had been his neck. His head hung from a few strands of muscle, gristle and skin. The creature was naked, veins and tendons ran into each other. It had skin like a decomposing whale washed up on the beach, a flat piggish face and bald wispy notes of hair. Its jaw was extended and, also like a shark, had rows of teeth jammed into its gums.

It looked at me with black swinish eyes. It took another bite out of poor Yusuf's corpse and let what little was left drop to the floor.

The only reason I didn't drop my sword in horror and disgust was because I hadn't drawn it. I tripped out of the house into the village awash with moonlight. I kept my eyes focused on the door whispering suras from the Koran I thought I'd long forgotten, those I had heard could protect a traveler from djinn. I tried to steel myself. It worked. The cold hunting logic thumped into my head, 'no sense running from a wolf, it's faster than you.' I remembered the words of my aunts telling stories of how even the most vicious ghoul or shaytan, ones who rejected all the religions of the book, could be wounded and even killed by iron.

I could hear the creature take easy steps out of the hut into the doorway. It knew it had all the time it needed.

Once I managed to wrestle my sword out of its scabbard, I kept the blade low to hide how it shivered in my hand and so if I had to cut with it, I could put my entire body weight behind it.

The ghoul had to stoop to get through the doorway. I tried not to look directly at it, but I couldn't help myself be drawn into its ill-proportioned limbs held together by ropy cables of grey muscles. Every digit on its hand ended with a nail filthy and hardened like a claw. The shape of its face and jaw meant it couldn't grin, but baring its row upon row of fish hook teeth designed to drag its prey deeper into its gullet more than made up for that deficiency. It hit me like a cannon ball. Any thought that I might fight this creature was blown apart. It had crossed the distance between us and pinned me to the ground, I heard ribs snap under the pressure and the wind was forced out of my body. I drew a dagger, stabbed it into its arm over and over with every bit of strength I could muster. Rotten black blood seeped out of the wound over my face into my mouth and nostrils gagging me with the foul stench. If the creature felt the knife it didn't show it. It leaned forward, unhinging its jaw with those rows of teeth descending.

A bow twanged in the dark. An arrow punched clean through the creature and embedded itself in the ground. A grapple attached to the arrow by a length of chain snagged itself in the creature's body, tethering it to the ground.

A horse and rider followed the arrow out of the dark, a horn bow in the riders hand. He fired again and the ghoul found itself with another hook and chain fastening it to the earth. The ghoul span round to confront its new aggressor. I took the chance to worm my way out from under its grip and crawl through the mud out of its reach. The rider circled the ghoul firing his chained arrows at it from a different angle each time and though the ghoul tried to charge the rider it found itself more and more imprisoned by each arrow that punched through its body. The ghoul roared with what to a first lesson sounded like frustration and anger, but in which was contained a note of fear.

Safely out of the creature's reach, I looked upon my saviour. He was clad in back armour, layers of scale and cain mail in the style of an Anatolian Sipahi. His sword was a curved kılıç and his bow was the same stubby Anatolian bow I used, across his back was a one-handed Damascus steel axe with a crescent head and pick point. It was his horse that impressed me most, such a gigantic horse I have rarely seen. With its armoured headgear and mail flanks, had I seen it from a distance, I could easily have mistaken it for one of the Sultan's rhinoceros.

The rider jumped off his horse, seemingly unhindered by his armour, his sword in his hand. He walked up to the monster to deliver a killing blow. The ghoul snarled and cowered at the approach of the rider straining against the chains gnashing those hideous rows of teeth.

Whether one of the chains came loose or the ghoul was employing some primitive cunning, I don't know, but when the Sipahi stepped within a sword's reach the creature lashed out. It batted the Sipahi's weapon out of his hand with its talons and lunged. The grapples pulled apart the ghoul's flesh like rotten paper, but it didn't seem to notice. Free of some of its shackles, it sunk its teeth into the

Sipahi's shoulder the rows of teeth screeched as they sunk into his armour. Like a dog with a cat between its jaws, the ghoul started to thrash. Slamming the rider into ground while the jaws ground from side to side like a saw. If the rider hadn't had his brains dashed out on the inside of his helm, it would not have be long before those teeth opened up his armour and feasted on the meat beneath.

From where my courage came, I cannot say, maybe it was from Allah or perhaps a survival instinct, but I moved. I sprung up and ran forward, bringing my sword down on the ghoul with all my might. Its flesh parted easily, but my blade got stuck there as if I'd bought an axe down into waterlogged wood. The creature roared, dropping the Sipahi out of its jaws. It tried to swing one of its hands at me, the claws darting towards my eyes.

Had the assault connected, it would have ripped my head from my shoulders.

But the claw did reach me. It had been stopped at a hand's span from my face, those filthy razor sharp claws a finger's distance from my eye. The Sipahi stood up straight as if he had nearly risen from a nap. The ghoul's arm was caught in his mail fist. Between the slits in his helmet I could have sworn that the Sipahi's eyes glowed red. Though the ghoul pulled and strained, the Sipahi fist didn't pop-open, rather the opposite, finger by finger he ratcheted the ghoul's arm back.

Easily, as if time were his to dispose of, the Sipahi reached over his shoulder and unslung the axe from his back. I watched him swing it, pick first into the ghoul's skull. That was not enough to kill it it, which still squirmed and pulled at the chains, at the axe embedded in its skull and the hand clamped to its arm. That it could move, that it could fight, punctured with arrows, gashed by my sword and with a spike lodged in its brain was testimony to the unholy energy that was keeping the best moving. But now its snapping jaws and tense muscles seemed bent on escape, not attack. That didn't help it. The Sipahi twisted the axe, wrenched the arm back and exposed the black throbbing veins on the creature's neck.

The solid metal of his helmet opened up like a curtain. I saw the Sipahi's lips, blue and dead. His jaw unhinged like a snake about to swallow a rat and I saw a pair of elongated canines. The Sipahi bit down on the ghoul's neck, the dark blood oozed down the chin of the Sipahi and fell in think splotches on his armour. The Sipahi drank like a nomad in the desert coming across a spring. He did not breathe or move, just gulped his throat passing the foul slime deep into his body. When the ghoul was spent, its body limp in his hands, he pulled the axe out of its skull and lopped off its head.

He turned and looked at me. The bloody mouth spoke in the perfumed Turkish of the Balkans, "Even the blood of ghouls can nourish." The Sipahi pulled off his helmet. I recognised him instantly. "Radu Bey." I said dropping to a knee. In my head I spoke his other names, Radu cel Frumos, the beautiful, the Sultan's Dragon, the younger Dracula.

"My brother will do more of these things, unleash more of these creatures and within himself he has great and terrible power. He will use all the guile and the blood in his veins to blunt us, but they will only make us stronger. Until he is forced to kneel before us, humbled. I will make this thing happen. Young Aḳıncı", he turned to look at me, the red eyes cut deep into my soul, my blood thumped in my ears, threatening to swoon me, but I met his gaze. "Today the ghoul has taught you defeat and humiliation."

I could not deny that it was true.

"What will you do about it? Are you the kind of warrior willing to rise above your shame, above death, this night to become something beyond human, to serve the Sultan in a new, more glorious form, to stand at my side when we cut the still living head from Vlad the Impaler and send it to our Sultan, preserved in honey so it can be exposed to the sun on the walls of Constantinople?"

He scooped up what was left of the ghoul's blood still leaking from its neck stump between cupped hands and offered it to me. Before it had leaked into my mouth it had tasted of rot and sickness, but now it smelled sweet and intoxicating like a mix of wine and opium.

I answered, "Yes."

THE CHILDREN OF LAMIA

by
Jacob Floyd

Beneath the floors of the abandoned Eastern Cemetery chapel sat five coffins and a sarcophagus. The coffins belonged to the children of Lamia, the dreaded half-serpent, half-woman vampire. The sarcophagus belonged to the 1400-year-old monster herself. No one suspected their presence in the city, not until Helen saw her; and then she found them and plotted to destroy them.

Ever since she watched Lamia slither into her bedroom and steal her beloved Carlos from their bed, she vowed this vengeance. Deep online research began, and she discovered the ancient abomination was once a Libyan princess, loved by Zeus. Together, she and the philandering god had five children. Though Hera was used to her unfaithful husband's weakness for lusting after human women, falling in love was intolerable. In a fit of goddess rage, she destroyed the children and cursed Lamia to be the coiling creature she was now. Zeus, in an attempt to return Lamia to her original form, succeeded in making the curse worse. Thanks to his thoughtless meddling with powers he did not understand, Lamia then had to feed on the blood of humans.

After a century or so, Lamia accidentally discovered her ability to shape shift. Angered by her new outward appearance, she uttered a curse to Hera; a sudden burst of lightning ripped the sky, and Lamia once again had feet. Needless to say, she was elated at this discovery as she believed she had transformed back into the princess she used to be. That she had either prolonged life or immortality had already occurred to her, and the thought of eternity in that hideous serpentine form made her long for death.

As she slumbered on the first night of her new discovery, she awoke famished, and when she rose out of bed, she dropped to the floor and slithered away in the dark. For many minutes she cried out, terrified that she would remain as the beast forever. Having her hopes dashed, she continued into the night and fed well. With her hunger sated, her coiling body began to form into legs; in minutes, her lower half had returned to normal and she was whole once more. Thus came the realization that the snake body was needed for hunting, but she could spend the rest of the time as her original self.

Not until a botched hunt had she realized she could turn others into blood drinkers. A man she had taken (she took only men) stabbed her with a silver knife while she was feeding on him and it burned her terribly. After the assault, she recoiled and the man fled. The next night, when she woke beneath the home of a farmer she had slain, she found the man standing outside. Her human form still dominated, and she looked the man in the eyes, and he knelt, saying he was there to serve her. The man became her first disciple.

Over time it became apparent the man needed to feed in the same manner as she did – on the blood of the living – and as long as he performed the tasks she assigned him, he was rewarded with the blood she did not drink. Sometime later, she determined the man was useless and killed him with a silver knife.

Lamia grew lonely, lamenting the loss of her children. The wretched Hera had deprived her of the joys of motherhood, and even in this wretched state she still felt that loss. It was during one of these bouts that she realized she was capable of claiming children of her own, and so she did.

These dark offspring were children she'd stolen from villagers and turned. No matter who they once were, they became devoted to her, and she to them. They hunted for her and scouted her prey. Though they were all capable of existing in daylight—including Lamia—they were strongest at night. However, the children did not necessarily need their vampire strengths to survive, for she saw to it they had all they needed. Due to this, the arrangement became that some of the children would slumber with her, and others would search the nearby towns for prime game.

At one time, there were as many as fifteen children, but it was always inevitable that someone would catch on to what she was. Once knowledge about vampires was more prevalent, it became difficult for her to slink about and snag unsuspecting victims. There were times when one or two kills attracted attention and alerted townsfolk to her true nature. This often resulted in some of her children being slain.

But the modern age was much better. It was almost like the old days when no one knew about her. Oh, they knew much about vampires now, but everyone believed them to be a myth, especially in the more, as they say, "civilized" countries where virtually no one believed in such things; and, that included religion, which aided Lamia since religious artifacts were repellant to her thanks to Hera and Zeus.

Not all of this could be found online or in the library, of course. Helen had to consult experts. A man in Iowa who went simply by the name Dark One had come highly recommended despite his juvenile moniker. Helen had consulted known scholars on such legends and mythologies, and they all pointed her to Dark One, who was an anonymous online fountain of information on the occult, supernatural, and legends of zombies, werewolves, and vampires. Dark One offered his own knowledge and sent her many links to tomes that were more underground and went much deeper than the mainstream literature she previously studied – writings which more or less treated the entire subject as a joke or campfire tale. Dark One's references were not only written from a believer's point of view, but some were penned with great urgency. Some claimed to have witnessed Lamia steal a man or child close to them. Helen had every reason to believe a few of the accounts because they matched hers perfectly.

On the night she took Carlos, Lamia slithered through the open window and wrapped her tail around him, slid him slowly from the bed, and dragged him into the night. A mist lay over the room, and it forced Helen into a paralyzed state. Initially, she had believed it to be a dream; however, when she woke and found Carlos not in bed, she knew. Even though she searched the entire house for him, she knew he had been stolen by that monster.

Running out into the night with no shoes and just a housecoat thrown over her sleeveless nightgown, the woman went in pursuit of the demon creature, only to lose it a couple of blocks from the cemetery. When she rounded the corner onto the city road where the graveyard was located, she saw only a woman in a dress walking down the sidewalk with a man next to her. Knowing Eastern was abandoned, she automatically assumed the beast had gone there; if it had not, she concluded it would have slipped into the sewer. Either way, she vowed to find out where this creature nested.

After learning everything she could about Lamia, she camped out on the corner across from the cemetery at sunset. Nearly an hour after the sky had gone black, a woman in a long white dress emerged from the graveyard and walked down the street. Helen followed. Upon passing beneath a train bridge, she watched the woman morph into the serpent that had taken Carlos. Needing to observe no further, Helen returned home to plan her attack.

There was but one place something like the Lamia could hide in Eastern Cemetery – beneath the abandoned chapel. Helen was nearly certain that's where she would find the creature. So, on the day she bore witness to the abomination's metamorphosis, she hit up every knife-selling shop she could find in order to obtain a silver blade; she ended up purchasing a silver short sword with a sheath. Helen was no small woman; she was strong with muscular arms and shoulders; wielding the sword would be no hard task.

The weapon lay across her back as she took the alleys and side roads to the cemetery. Sunset was about two hours away; the beast should still be sleeping. An afternoon invasion was out of the question because the block was busy at that time; a woman with a sword on her back venturing into the cemetery would likely gain unwanted attention, not to mention the possibility of being spotted breaking into the old chapel. Though the building sat back far enough to not be visible from the road, joggers often ran the Eastern paths, and many people walked their dogs there. Early evening was best since the streets were quiet around that time.

Standing against the side of a gentrified apartment building facing the graveyard, Helen looked both ways down the avenue. Two cars passed without incident. No one was outside, so she stepped from the corner onto the sidewalk and then crossed the empty street. The gold-orange glow of the late afternoon sun spread across the bars of the cemetery gate, which stood open as she crossed the threshold. The grass inside was high.

No one owned this land anymore. Eastern had long been abandoned and left to rot by the city. It took years before the old chapel was finally boarded up. The only opening that remained was where the bodies were once delivered for cremation. The heavy sliding wooden door still remained and was mostly intact.

The first section of Eastern was a straight concrete road running east. After walking about a quarter mile, the road curved north for a short stretch before turning east once more. This lead to the chapel in the back and was isolated from any eyes on the street. Once Helen was on that route, she drew her sword and held it to her side, letting it brush the grass. The small green blades fell to the silver one she held. In a few minutes, the cinder-block chapel came into view.

Helen came to the front of the building and looked around, listening for any sound of movement. When she was sure all was well, she placed the sword on the ground before her, lifted her arms – hard biceps flexing against the leather of her trench coat – and removed the sheath from her back. Next, she shrugged off the long jacket, folded it, and laid it on the ground next to the sheath. Then, to ensure her vision would remain unhindered, she took the ponytail holder from her wrist and wrapped her flaxen blonde hair into a tight ponytail. As she was doing this, she felt her muscles tightening; she was ready for the fight.

Helen picked up her sword and headed around the side of the building, walked down the ramp, and stood before the sliding door. As she stared, feeling her breath enter and leave her lungs, she thought of the darkness that was on the other side. This moment could lead to her death. As brave as she was, as strong as she was, she was still only human; she was not an immortal monster with talons and mighty fangs. Upon sliding this door open, she could be walking into her tomb.

But Carlos was in there, and she wasn't going to leave him to the wicked whims of Lamia.

Helen's fingers wrapped around the handle; she took one step back and slid the door open. The weather-beaten wood ground against the tracks, making a sick sound of struggle that threatened to shatter the door to splinters. The door wobbled and bucked, and Helen had to use both hands, but she finally forced it open, and that's how she left it as she entered. If a fast getaway was needed, she didn't want the door to impede her.

Judging by the stink of blood, Helen decided the nest was nearby. The lower level was dark, but the flashlight on her phone provided all the light she'd need. Ahead she saw five small coffins and one large sarcophagus sitting across the room. Two of the coffins were open and empty. Lamia's scouts must have been at work, no doubt looking for another Carlos to steal.

Before opening one of the other three, she decided to search the area for her man. Dead or alive, she needed to know where he was. The building didn't cover much ground, so she didn't have to travel far before she found him chained to a table against the wall furthest from the nest.

Quickly, she rushed to his side. In the light of the phone she could see his eyes were closed and he looked ill; his face was white and nearly drained of life, but he was breathing. After setting down her phone, she administered four light slaps to wake him. When he saw her, his eyes widened. "Helen, you found me. How did you know?"

"Educated guess. Now, keep quiet. I'm going to get you out of here."

Helen rested the sword against the table and tugged at the chains but they wouldn't budge. She began looking around for something sharp to pick the lock and found a few items that didn't work. As she tried to jimmy a shackle loose with one of them, Carlos spoke. "Is it dark outside yet?"

"Not yet, but we don't have much time."

"You have to get us out of here before she wakes up, or she'll feed on us both."

"No she won't, because I'm going to chop the bitch's head off."

"With what?"

"I have a sword with a silver blade."

"Will that work?"

"Yes. I've done some reading on her. When we get out of here, I'll tell you all about her."

Helen gave up on picking the lock and found a mallet. This would undoubtedly work, but the amount of noise the act of bashing the shackles apart would produce would likely wake at least one of the demons.

"Let me take care of them. When I'm done, I'll break you out."

Carlos shook his head. "What are you going to do?"

"Kill them while they sleep."

"Two of them are gone. They'll be back before dark."

"Then I'll have to kill the others while I have the advantage."

"Helen…"

But it was too late. Helen pocketed her phone, grabbed her sword, and was heading towards the nearest coffin. After a brief pause, she popped it open and looked down on Lamia's sleeping child.

Remember, this is no child.

The sword suddenly felt very heavy in her hands as she lifted it, tip down, over the sleeping vampire. The sword trembled just before she rammed it into the creature's heart. With a quick yank she pulled back the blade. The creature's eyes and mouth were already open as it shrieked in its death throes. Helen slammed the coffin shut and turned her back. To her left were the two other occupied coffins. Both had begun to shake as the creatures inside awoke. Helen reached for the lid of the closest just as it flew open. Another child sat up and looked at her, its red eyes lit. Before it could rise, Helen swiped her sword at its neck. The blow almost took the head off, but it lolled to the side where it was still connected by a few strings of flesh. The vampire rocked back and forth, its nearly-severed head rolling and flopping around violently before it finally fell off. The creature convulsed several times as it slowly melted away.

The coffin behind Helen opened up and the other child rose to its feet, screeching. Helen spun and sliced its leg, tearing an enormous gash. The beast cried out and leapt at her with its arms outstretched. Helen fell back with the sword held up in front of her; she landed on her back and the vampire impaled itself on her sword. Not wanting to lose the weapon, she lifted her foot and tried to push the creature away, but it burst into flames and began melting. Helen let go of the sword and backed away; she then stood as the child rose. In one quick motion, she reached out for the handle, pulled it towards her, and landed a flying kick into the dying monster's chest. The impact pulled loose the sword and sent Lamia's child sailing back onto the sarcophagus.

As the dying vamp lay kicking and screaming, Lamia woke from her slumber. There was a rumble from within the sarcophagus as the heavy stone lid began to move aside. Helen quickly stood in preparation to kill the fiend as the child melted at her feet, arms and legs degenerating to mush, eyeballs and tongue oozing from the face, the skin sliding away and pooling on the floor as the creature became a colorful bubbling stew.

The lid flew back and a scream erupted from within the sarcophagus. Lamia shot up and out, flying over Helen's head and landing between her and where Carlos lay. When their eyes met, Lamia hissed, her mouth already growing those long, dangerous fangs; her nails becoming flesh-rending talons, and her legs slowly melting together. The red eyes now before Helen were much larger and far brighter than those she saw previously.

"You killed my children."

"And I'm going to kill you." Helen lifted her sword with both hands, ready to strike the tall creature down.

A chilling growl rolled slowly from Lamia's throat. "I will rip you to shreds."

Helen held out her weapon. “Come and try me.”

Lamia’s serpentine lower half made an unnerving squishy sound as she slithered forward. Helen struck out with the sword, aiming for the creature’s heart. Lamia swiped the blow to the side with her long talons, making a loud clang on the blade. After a couple of seconds, she hesitated and hissed, holding her hand. The blade nicked her, and smoke drifted from the wound.

Helen smiled. “Yeah, silver, bitch.”

Lamia hissed again and came forth with her arms outstretched and her talons splayed. Helen swung the sword but Lamia dodged, her powerful arms then embraced her attacker; one hand held the sword arm and the other Helen’s throat, the talons slowly pushing into the flesh. Upon her serpent form, Lamia stood around eight feet tall, but she lowered herself to peer with her red eyes into Helen’s blues.

“Why have you come?”

“To kill you, obviously,” said Helen through struggled breaths.

“Is that your man I’ve taken?”

“It is, and I’m taking him back.”

Lamia smiled, and the points of her top fangs seemed to gleam in the growing darkness. “Why throw away your life for some useless man? Surely he is not worth it.”

“Yeah, he’s not a vain, philandering god, so he’s not exactly your type.”

“You keep up the courage even in the face of death. I admire that. Unfortunately, I will destroy you, but before I do, I'll allow you to watch me tear your man apart."

While Lamia wasted time gloating over Helen, the would-be demon slayer managed to reposition the sword in her hand; now holding it as one would a dagger, she managed to push it into Lamia's arm, causing her to let go. Helen then rammed the sword into Lamia's side, stabbing it just slightly into the tough hide. Lamia screamed and backed away. Smoke rose all around her and the redness of her eyes turned to a deeper hue. The light outside was quickly dying and the monster was harder to see. Helen pulled the phone from her pocket and quickly switched on the flashlight, momentarily blinding Lamia.

This hesitation allowed Helen the opportunity to gain her proper fighting stance and come for Lamia, though she hesitated as well after getting an eyeful of the enemy she was facing. Lamia's torso and upper arms were ripped with muscle; her snake half was thick and powerful. Helen had to strike fast if she was to stand a chance.

The sword rose towards the creature's neck. Lamia managed to bring her arm up just in time to block the blow, and the blade took a chunk of her forearm instead of her face.

As Lamia screamed and held her arm, taking her eyes off of Helen, the slayer went in for the kill. With her sword held before her, tip pointed upwards, Helen charged, aiming for the heart. Just before the blade entered Lamia's chest, something hit Helen hard from the side, throwing her across the room and slamming her into the north wall. Without thinking, she swung the sword around to chop at whatever had hit her, and she dug the blade edge in deep. The attacker squealed; it was one of the other children. When it backed away, Helen drove the sword into its throat and it began to melt and thrash about.

Helen was then lucky enough to catch a quick glimpse of another child coming up behind the dying one. Flying out of the darkness, the child's red eyes rapidly approached Helen. The hiss of the creature was horrifying, but it did not halt her; she leapt to her feet just in time. The child hit the wall and Helen spun around with the sword held out and swiped off the creature's head.

As she watched the child die, she did not see Lamia coming up behind her. Her phone had fallen to the floor with the light still on, and Carlos saw Lamia's approach.

"Helen! Behind you!"

Helen turned just in time to be tackled and pushed out of Carlos' line of sight. Both woman and creature screamed and grunted in the darkness below Eastern's abandoned chapel. Scuffling, body blows, and items falling to the ground could be heard across the lower level. Lamia screeched a couple of times. Then, a loud metallic twang was heard, followed by Helen's scream. The fighting then stopped and Carlos waited for a quite some time, but no one ever came into the light. The phone eventually died while he was waiting, and he passed out soon after.

When Carlos awoke, it was pitch black except for the moon shining in the small window above him. "Helen?" he whispered. Then louder: "Helen?"

Carlos began to cry. Most certainly she was dead. Likely Lamia too, but he didn't care. What did he now have that would make him care about freedom? Without Helen, he wanted to die as well.

Then some shuffling brought him around. Fear began to take him as he listened for either a hiss or the sound of Lamia's moist tail moving along the floor. To his utter relief, Helen emerged from the other side of the chapel, covered in blood and looking ragged.

"Helen! Are you okay?"

Carlos' savior walked over to him and placed her cold hand on his cheek. "I think so."

"Is she dead?"

Helen nodded. "She bled all over me."

"Help me out of here."

"I'm starving, Carlos."

"Then let me out and we can go home."

"No, I don't think you understand. That thing – she bled on me."

Carlos shook his head. "You are right. I don't understand. What does that have to do with…"

Suddenly, Helen leaned over, feeling her teeth growing in her mouth, and plunged them into Carlos' neck. The man screamed and kicked, then Helen rose back up with blood staining her lips and chin. Carlos looked on in horror as the eyes of the woman he loved began to glow a deep red.

"I swallowed her blood, and she sank her teeth into me just before she died. Now, I'm starving."

Helen leaned over again and began to feed. Carlos never saw her legs blend together, and he never heard the squishy sound she made leaving the chapel that night.

PARASITES: A TALE OF ROUTE 66

by

B. J. Thrower

I prefer to meet my victims at amiable gatherings where they're relaxed, or even stoned. Music festivals are among my favorite places, but to be honest, it never matters where I am: in a stadium with 50,000 baseball fans, or an airport parking lot, or on a desolate country road. After I finish with them, the imp of whichever particular night appears, and I give him whatever body I have.

Tonight on the Guthrie Green in downtown Tulsa, the pounding outdoor concert suddenly reminds me of Vinson's fist smashing my face. I saw him last where he stayed with the cactus and scorpions when he wasn't in a daytime cave, or stashing himself out of sight in town, in the midnight desert east of the Pacific coast.

When I asked about the imps, Vinson the Elder squinted his red, sunset eyes at me. It displeased him, but if anyone knew where the imps came from, or how long they've existed, it was him. All I know for certain is what I'm most familiar with: how they're linked to us like parasites.

Vinson was unfriendly whenever I sought him out, but he was impressive; tall and barrel-chested with powerful arms, the oldest of us I'd ever met. He liked to wear rustic robes, with hoods to hide his face, and had long silver hair. I thought he looked like a medieval monk, but he was a monk who could break me in half with those gigantic hands. I'd seen the chains of silver, gold or jeweled crosses under his robes, yet he wasn't a believer. Vinson hunted priests or other religiously inclined hoodoo men and women risen in the ranks of the liberal Protestant churches in this modern time of gender equality and its various incarnations.

Vinson had a beef with the self-styled cohorts of deities because he'd been *nailed*, not tied, to a wooden cross, and roasted by some miserable rat of a priest somewhere in Europe centuries ago. He survived, of course, and no doubt taken revenge on the arsonist who burned his flesh.

But like all of us, Vinson delivered the dead bodies he created to our parasites, the imps; bodies for disposal which would otherwise rot in plain sight of Mankind, be pondered and investigated. Exposed corpses were too dangerous for us, a tiny minority stalking the world of fragile mortals. Buried bodies were discovered too often. And new technology? iPhones with cameras, still shots or videos uploaded for eternity on the internet highway revealed us to the billions of spiteful people on the planet, the villagers with pitchforks.

Vinson had cuffed me for my impertinent question. Through the ringing in my ears, muttering more to himself than to me, "Once . . . when the imp's door opened, I heard gears shifting like boulders, and the rush of foul drainage water.

I saw the masonry towers of windmills, and the cloth sails—nay, not wooden slats—and the caps turning in mist, powered by wind that couldn't exist . . . there shouldn't have been any fog!" He fixed me with a baleful glare. "There was a field of them, gristmills for grain, pumps for flooded fields next to my village when I was a lad.

"It is different for each of us, these spaces where imps dwell. What we glimpse or overhear inside their doors depends on the age of the world *we* lived in as humans." He poked my chest with an index finger. "When the imps speak, I forbid you to answer! Do ya hear me, Youngster?"

And then he hit me again, blasting the side of my face with his enormous fist so hard I ended up flat on my back, cursing at him from the hardscrabble while he spared a few more seconds to stare down at me before spurning my company.

But I couldn't let it go. In Texas in the aftermath of Harvey, in the stinking, electricity-free killing zone of a pitch black Houston alley, after a blood orgy with my *cholo*, Rico, I suggested we go to the imps together to deliver the bodies of the two meth addicts we'd murdered. We hunted well as a pair, and never squabbled over victims. I'd enjoyed his company until he exclaimed, "*Amigo*, you are *loco*! The imps, you don't wanna mess with them."

Disappointed, I asked, "You won't try it with me?"

Rico was the one who'd explained Vinson's history to me. He was bulky with black hair to his waist, physically commanding not unlike myself, though I was blonde, with hair as long as his. He'd been one of us since Santa Ana's war with the Texicans, before Texas (Northern Mexico) was overrun with white settlers, the slavers and Comanche-hunters who'd fought over this land with the native peoples, including him.

In the modern concrete labyrinth, his eyes glowed like burning cherries pulsating with fresh sustenance. I imagined my eyes did the same. He laid a hand on my shoulder, saying with compassion, "There are some things even we may never know."

I flung his hand off. "We're immortal. Who else should?"

"We are immortal with limitations, in some circumstances, severe limitations. We may yet die, and to speculate of the imps is forbidden for a reason. We shouldn't speak of them."

"Fine," I replied angrily."But you can at least share with me what you know. What you've heard."

Promptly: "Nothing."

"I don't believe you! Have you ever spoken to an imp?"

In his hesitation, I saw that he had. Rico shrugged. "Of course. Who among us has not? Sometimes I forget, I reply when they ask for the toll. But I have never questioned them, and I never will."

"They won't tell me their names," I said, churlish about it.

"Perhaps they have no names," he replied. "Whatever they do behind their doors is darker than we can imagine."

"That's a lot of darkness!" I chided him. "You're a lapsed Catholic, Rico, full of superstition."

He grabbed my face and kissed my cheeks. His fangs grazed my lips. "I fear I will never see you again if you persist. Do you not recognize the threat? *Se nota en sus ojos, amigo, sus ojos*, it's in their *eyes*."

"Hey."

I look up. My next victim has come to me tonight. While recalling my past, I couldn't help notice her making a beeline toward me from the corner of my eye. It was a free annual music festival this weekend at the Guthrie Green, a newer urban park in the Greenwood Arts District lined with trees and shrubs. She had apparently spotted me away from the covered stage where I sat on a bench watching all the juicy mortals go by.

I smile at her, a minimal smile to hide my incisors. "Hey, yourself." Usually, I don't learn their names, but she expected me to ask. "What's your name?"

"Rochelle." Silence until she laughs, demanding, "Who are you, man?"

"Cal." I've had many names just as meaningless, but I liked the heaviness of the beer in her laughter, the streaks of Irish green, pretty-purple and dark blue in her brunette hair. She was small and trim and eager for my company.

"I think you're too far from the stage, Cal," she says.

"And?"

Hands on her hips. "Don't you want to be closer?"

"With you? Yes." I stand. She clasps my hand, never noticing how cool my skin is. I spend the next two hours watching her jump to the music; enthusiastic leaps to musical rhythms, her death-dance. I jumped, too, for appearances' sake.

When the band takes a break before the final hour of the concert, she claims my arm. Musical echoes in my ears, I stroll south with her along Boston Avenue, then cross East Brady Street. We continue on the sidewalk along the west side of the Woody Guthrie Center, then swing into the back alley where more murals are painted on the brick. Rochelle thinks I'm going to kiss her, and in a way, I do.

Her blood is bitter tasting, the flavor of regret—and I knew I should have let her go. I've spared people before, a few of the multitudes who've sacrificed everything to me. But I'd been incapable of sparing anyone over the past year, since the imps don't come without delivery of a body. The imps draw me now toward what I most desire to learn, a swelling compulsion bursting at seams both invisible—or defined, by Vinson's fist.

I'm the American lone wolf predator, and I usually keep to my territory along Interstate 40, crossing the country east to west and back, from sea to shining sea. Occasionally, my path deviates, and lately I've travelled old Route 66. Tulsa is my hometown, where 66 is called 11th Street, advertised as a tourist attraction of historical interest. Along Route 66, the famous plaster Blue Whale outside Catoosa between here and Joplin always bemused me. The people are affectionate about it, when to me it's tawdry and cheaply constructed. I recall when I was a human boy, my grandmother told me *her* mother had gone into labor with her in the old Will Rogers movie theater on the south side of 11th Street between Harvard and Yale. But it isn't ol' Will Rogers who stands above me at the moment, but the other famous Son of Oklahoma, Woody Guthrie.

Where we are on the west side of the two-story, red brick building of the Guthrie Center, we're in the shadows beneath Woody's mural—black on a mottled beige background, with white lettering: THIS LAND IS YOUR LAND. Woody in black clothes and pale faced, guitar strap hung over his left shoulder, looking north at the crosswalks painted on road tarmac.

Downtown Tulsa gleams around Rochelle and I in its art deco and contemporary insanity. Off to the south with windows like glycerin, the tower of the Williams Building, at one time the tallest building in the state, and an exact replica of the vanquished Twin Towers in Manhattan, except in height. Designed by the same architect, but only sixty stories, it managed to make a genuine urban landscape resembling those of other, larger cities than "Tulsey Town" was.

At this late hour, the city core bangs with train noises, with Saturday night music, with the flashing red lights of police cars as they stop to roust the homeless. After the bars close at 2 a.m., downtown Tulsa will diminish in sound for a couple of hours. Before then, the young and moneyed (or striving for money) with a few seniors mixed in, stroll around after dining at expensive or eclectic restaurants before they disappear into the music venues.

The people here had evolved from a dependency on the oil and gas dynasties of the past, who in their death throes made earthquakes rumble across the state by forcing wastewater into the bedrock, with the compliance of local politicians. These newer generations had found other niches for themselves, though the carnival barkers of the evangelicals still held sway. Yeah, ol' Woody wouldn't have liked the oil and gas companies much, but ol' Route 66 had led me here, the same as every road eventually did.

With Rochelle over my shoulders, I'll walk until the imp's door appears ahead of me, something only I can see. I can't predict how many steps I'll take, but wherever we tread after our nightly feasts, the imps wait for us. And so I tote her around the corner and down the sidewalk, keeping to the trees or shadows of the warm spring night, admiring the mural of Woody as I walk. The concert had started again, the music loud but now a block away.

Stabbing from the dark, crimson thorns of light outlined tonight's imp-door. Downtown vanishes in the red gloss, the bloody gloaming of it, as the music fades away. I trudge the corridor of unnatural light, with her as my silent companion.

Time shifts here, or nearly ceases to exist; it's difficult to judge. My right forearm is slung over

Rochelle's limp neck and I can see the watch on my wrist, illuminated inside this red tunnel. The second hand ticks busily in a circle, but the other hand on this watch—or of any other watch—never moves.

A bloom of white light as the door opens and slams shut. The imp of this particular night has come outside to greet me. I plod the rest of the way and stand in front of him with my problem, the girl.

He is small at barely four feet in height, identical to his brethren. He wears only a stiff leather apron to his filthy ankles, bringing to mind a tradesman, or a butcher. I think he's red, but that's because I've only seen them in this weird aura. His skin is old, wrinkled, potted with warts, hair sparse except in his elephantine ears. Barefoot, he has a demonic face, with angles like nails instead of bones.

His gnarled hand thrusts out and he says, "A piece of gold."

I adjust the weight and balance of Rochelle's body across my shoulders. Every imp asks for payment, as if the bodies aren't enough. From Vinson, the price is a single pubic hair; Rico crystal glassware; and from me, gold. I often find a snippet of gold on my victims, the final thing I steal from them. My price isn't even painful like Vinson's.

I say, "No gold tonight, Imp."

He grins. "No piece of gold, no delivery. Git yourself a shovel, Vampire, an' start diggin'." He laughs; apparently, I amuse him. He reaches backward and grasps the solid handle welded in the metal door. I stay him by holding up the gold ring I'd already wriggled off Rochelle's finger.

He snatches it from my hand. Biting it, he says, "I'll take her now, and I thank ye kindly." Normally, this concludes our nightly encounters: when an imp drags a body through the door, the red light is gone, and I am standing in the real world again.

I lay Rochelle on the ground but rest my boot on her neck. I tell myself that this is the night when my obsession overrules reason at last, here in my hometown. This is my particular night, I decide, not the imp's. "I don't think so." Behind him, there's a vague throb of machinery. "What is this place?"

"This? Why, this is *my* place."

"I—liked this girl, a little," I tell him, catching hold of his scrawny neck. "What will you do with her?"

"She will be processed." He offers no resistance, so I figure I'm correct that he can be killed.

"My name is Cal," I say. "What's yours?"

Instead of answering, he asks, "How long have you been a killer—Cal?"

I don't know why it surprises me when he uses my name. He's personalized me since.

I introduced myself, but perhaps it's because no other imp has addressed me like this. But I confess, "Twenty years."

He grins again. "Yer young to be bored with blood-suckin' and slaughter."

"I'm not necessarily bored," I reply, though it hadn't occurred to me before, in truth.

Gleefully: "Only the desperately bored trifle with an imp."

"Suppose I snap your neck, go inside, and see for myself?"

"You'll rue it," he declares. "Don't tarry, Cal! The sun comes."

"Time doesn't pass here. How do you know where the sun is?" I ask.

"I sense the heat," he answers. "And the sun, she always rises for vampires. Time ain't required."

His skin is desiccated; he seems not to be made of ordinary flesh. There's no blood in him, I realize. He's repulsive and offensive, like touching decay. I'm positive, since my hands are around his throat now. I tighten my grip. "She will be processed into what?"

Croaking, "Only those who ride the conveyor may know that, and they don't give a shit, cuz they're dead. The answer is at the end of the conveyor, Monster, beneath the threshers."

I pick him up and use his head as a battering ram against the door. He inexplicably laughs as his skull shatters to powder.

So, I've murdered an imp now, and I feel that it diminishes me, I feel weak. But at least I'll know.

I decide to take Rochelle inside; I stoop down and lift her in my arms. Together we open the door and step over the threshold. Independently, the door slams shut behind us.

Its lighting ordinary, the room is industrial, with aluminum siding adding a sheen to the walls.

It's deafening, with humping engines bashing my eardrums. A wide, vibrating, horizontal conveyor belt operates, so lengthy it vanishes in the distance of the room. *Lama-lama-lama,* it says. Except for where it turns on the roller shaft mechanism on this end of the room, it's covered by a funnel-like, steel hood. The odor of grease is cloying and repugnant to my over-sensitive nose.

I'm surprised such a relatively crude piece of machinery represents my age, as Vinson claimed. I might have expected more HAL-9000, or an automated factory floor with robots. But if this is how the imps dispose of bodies, then it must mean that Vinson's windmill pulverized his victims in the gristmills, then pumped whatever remained into the nearest water source—and either method left no trace.

But it isn't the only thing in the shiny room which surprises me.

"Well, my dear," I say to her, she wide-eyed, but not in amazement like me, "I guess you should be processed, anyway."

In order to reach the conveyor, I'm forced to wade into a pile of waist deep gold in front of me. The heap is high and substantial, like a dragon's hoard. Muscling my way through, I see trinkets, bracelets, watches, rings, reminding me of all the payments I've ever surrendered to the imps . . . *And so it is!,* I reason. Would Vinson find crude iron racks of short hair wigs, Rico a room of shimmering, deadly crystal? I had always assumed, *they'd* always thought each night brought a new imp, but are we all mistaken?

Shaking my head in wonder, I glance backwards and think I see two red, diamond eyes peering through the steel door from the other side. Dismissing the vision as a hallucination brought on by excitement or dread, I push through the sinkhole of gold.

Behind me out of reach, the door opens and closes again. "Hee-hee," the imp says.

I swivel awkwardly, and stare in disbelief that he's alive, that I was fooled by an illusion of death. I demand, "Who are you?"

His answer, "I am the single mirror in which you can see, Cal. This is what you truly look like."

Indoors, he's not red except for his beady eyes, but white, the color of a fish's belly. His lips curl. He has fangs now, like mine. Hoarse with alarm, I shout, "What—who made you?"

"You did!" he sneers. "Inside us there's duality, a schism of the soul and body in time. While you drink blood and prance and preen and prey, hiding from the sun, I collect payment and process the victims where I'm safe from the sun—but where I'm utterly alone, waiting for someone Outside to stake your chest and stuff your mouth with garlic. Bring a merciful end to my suffering."

I lurch out from the gold and drop Rochelle at the head of the conveyor, holding her on it by her belt, unsure about letting her go. When I turn toward him again, I notice my hands have become cramped and knotted. I'm no longer tall nor imposing, but short and dumpy. I'm becoming him, I see, and he—is becoming me, he's growing taller, into that part of me which is vital and wicked, with blonde hair to my ass. Rico was right! The threat was always there in his eyes, but they were my own eyes I did not recognize.

"I leave you here in this room of woe," he says, "to take your place Outside. It passes the time to count our gold, and in here, time is slow on our blackened soul, as slow as clotting blood."

"No!" I shout. "You'll stay!"

"No imp can stop me." He laughs. I'm laughing at myself.

Wearing the hated apron now, I release Rochelle. She travels the conveyor, entering the funnel of the long hood. He, the imp who is me, claimed there was an answer beneath the thresher blades. I can hear them, snicking and snacking, swishing, sharpened to a razor's edge as they sing through the air of my self-made damnation.

This is our hell then, in these rooms of our souls where we meet face-to-face, where we pay for our sins.

He's opened the door! The crimson light of the corridor dims and there's a hint of remembered music now beyond the horror in here, the culmination of our strange, violent, selfish life.

There are more ways for us to perish than by stake and garlic, but I must act quickly, for as my own imp I will be powerless, my agony ageless. My fangs are gone and my flabby lips quiver.

I climb aboard the conveyor belt—which isn't easy since I'm terribly short—lying on my back. Nearly fully formed, my imp's body is carried forward. The conveyor hums beneath me as I ride it. He roars in dismay as I slip under the maw of the steel funnel where he can't reach this part of himself.

And now only the threshers await us, and the final death that they will grant us. In the darkness ahead, I can hear them.

TAKE ME HOME TONIGHT

by

Troy Diffenderfer

Tonight was going to be the night Bobby talked to the girl with the pierced nose and red heels.

The first night he saw her, she had her head tilted back and her mouth hanging open, her black lipstick surrounding a set of perfect and tiny teeth. He wanted to know what she was laughing at. Her body seemed to shake in time with the punk band that was letting loose on stage.

Bobby spent the rest of the night casting furtive glances at her, capturing mental snapshots that created a timeline for the night. Click! There she was, smoking a cigarette and waiting in line for the restroom, one heel clicking impatiently on a sticky floor. Click! She was pushing through sweaty masses to the front of the stage. He followed her spiked Mohawk like a shark fin as she swam through the crowd. Click! There she was outside, stumbling out with the rest and pulling her leather jacket tight against herself as she walked into the darkness.

The second night he saw her, he worked up the nerve to talk to her . . .almost. For a week and a half, she was all he could think about. Bobby worked in IT in Santa Clarita, and with computers gradually taking off, he could afford to spend a few extra nights out on the town. By day, he was mild-mannered Robert, who wore ties and slacks, and had his hair carefully parted to one side. By night, he was Bobby, who made the commute down the interstate to prowl the thriving punk rock scene on sunset strip. He'd slide on his spiked leather boots, jeans with too many holes to count, an eye-catching band t-shirt, and head out (but not before putting a handful of grease in his hair).

Punk rock found Bobby at an early age when he was living back at home in New York. His parents were both Jewish, his mother a secretary and his father an accountant. With no siblings, Bobby was often left to find his own form of entertainment. Luckily, they lived a block away from a local record store.

While most kids spent time after school playing pickup basketball or riding their bikes through the abandoned construction sites, Bobby found a second home in the record shop. He was a quiet but attentive kid, which was exactly why the owner, Mr. Forsythe, took a liking to him. Mr. Forsythe turned out to be Alan Forsythe, who was somewhat of a local legend. Back in the 60s, Mr. Forsythe was known as one of the best drummers on the East Coast. While Ringo and Jon Bonham may have commandeered the spotlight, Alan Forsythe would go on to play drums on some of the most famous albums to come out of the 60s. Unlike many of the superstars of that time, Alan Forsythe hated the spotlight, which was why he decided to stop recording music and opened up a tiny record store in his own town.

Mr. Forsythe admired Bobby's naivety when it came to music, and he also admired his willingness to listen and learn even more. For years Bobby spent afternoons in that shop as Forsythe gave him a crash course on music. From Buddy Guy to Buddy Holly, Bobby quickly became enamored with not just the music itself, but the music scene as well.

Luckily, New York was quickly becoming a hub for emerging artists, especially emerging punk rock bands. Bobby was drawn to punk rock because he always felt like he was getting away with doing something illegal when he put those records on. He never strayed from the straight and narrow in school, but listening to the crash of guitars and the guttural screams made Bobby feel like it was he who was starting a rebellion.

As he grew older, he quickly realized that he could compartmentalize his love for punk rock. Not every rock lover had to be without a job or relying on drugs. Instead, he adopted a brand new persona, someone with the swagger and confidence to strike up a conversation with the girl in red heels.

Back at the club, Bobby caught sight of the girl for the second time. She still had those leather boots that snaked up her long legs and tucked neatly under a plaid skirt. Her hair was spiked once again, but this time it was bleach blonde.

Checking his hair once more in the bar mirror, he ordered two Jack and Cokes. He had never met the girl, but he just knew that was the kind of drink she'd enjoy. The band playing that night was a local favorite, so he had to muscle his way around the tightly packed crowd. He rehearsed in his head what he'd say. "Hi", was too bland; he'd come off as a tool bag. "Hey", was too nonchalant. She'd probably think he was trying to be too cool. He decided on, "Those are some kickass boots!" He figured that a compliment was a great icebreaker, and complimenting her boots would be more original than complimenting her eyes or hair.

Bobby was just about to slide into her vision with drinks in hand when a much larger man cut him off. Now, Bobby was well over six feet tall, but he was more of the sinewy, gangly type. This guy was around the same height, but his size seemed to absorb some of the light into the room. Suddenly this muscular shadow had eclipsed the woman, and he watched as the man leaned down towards her. Bobby couldn't see what they were saying, but he did notice the woman stand up on her tiptoes and whisper something in his ear. The man put a tree trunk of an arm around her waist and guided her towards the back of the crowd.

"Welp, another one bites the dust," Bobby mumbled to himself, and quickly drank both drinks before settling in for the rest of the show.

The third night he saw the girl, his life changed. It was almost a month after the last time he saw her, and to be honest, he had forgotten about her. Hollywood Boulevard wasn't a place where you eased into things. Whether it was drinking or a new relationship, people went headfirst into whatever they were getting into that night, which was why during that last month, he'd had his fair share of one-night stands and fuzzy mornings.

It was a Saturday night, always his favorite. To play the Whiskey on a Saturday meant that you were going places. At that time, Hollywood Boulevard was the place where bands made a name for themselves. If you had hits on the radio, most likely the crowd at the Whiskey heard them first. Saturdays at the Whiskey also meant that everyone was at the top of their game. Mohawks were extra tall, and piercings were a little more eye-catching.

Bobby already had a nice buzz going, along with a steady warmth that trickled into a sweat as the night went on. Being at a punk rock show was unlike anything he'd ever experienced. The crowd melted together into a mass of sweat and energy. His eyes were closed and he was enjoying the ringing in his ears as the band on stage led the crowd through a chaotic ritual of headbanging and jostling bodies.

He felt an arm snake through and hook onto the crook of his arm. He looked down to see the woman in the red heels flashing a smile at him. Her Mohawk was trimmed down. It was now just a stripe of red that ran front to back and matched her heels perfectly.

"These guys are killer!" she yelled, enunciating each syllable so he could hear her better.

"Nice shoes!" he yelled back, leaning down to bridge the sound gap. He gave himself an internal high five for finally being able to use his opening line.

"Why thank you, I'm Ana," she said, giving his arm a squeeze.

"I'm Bobby, can I get you a drink? Jack and Coke?"

"How'd you know?" she asked sheepishly. "Have you been spying on me?"

"Have I been flying? Well, once when I was little we went to Disney World."

"No! I said have you ever . . .never mind. Yes, I would LOVE a drink!" she said, screaming into his ear.

Bobby nodded and quickly returned with two Jack and Cokes.

"Let's take these to the back. I'm gonna lose my voice if I keep yelling at you," Ana said.

As they headed towards the back, Bobby spotted the bearded guy that he had seen Ana with the second time they crossed paths. He was sitting in the corner and nursing a beer. He seemed to be gripping the edge of the table as if he was afraid he was going to fall off at any time. His eyes were sunken and his flesh seemed to sag off of his face.

Bobby figured it took a truly dedicated music fan to still continue rockin' even though he was obviously dealing with some kind of illness. He didn't even notice that Ana had grabbed Bobby's hand as she led the way down to the basement. You were only allowed in the basement if you were a regular, which they both fortunately were. Back in the day, the basement was a speakeasy that sold whiskey during the prohibition era. Bobby always imagined mobsters and politicians chewing the fat down here and sipping on high-end liquor.

These days, the owner converted it into a lounge area. The walls were lined with vinyl, and anyone who'd like to could throw on a record and enjoy a cocktail on one of the many leather couches. Tonight, everyone was occupied with the band onstage, so Ana and Bobby had the place to themselves. They each sipped on their drinks while taking turns putting records on, trying to one up each other by playing obscure artists and rattling off facts about the bands. Bobby had to hand it to her: she certainly wasn't a poser. She could recite every album The Clash had put out and even the year they were released. She knew which labels each band was signed with, and even threw on a few artists that he'd never even heard of.

"Yes, but don't you think Billy Idol is a little . . .boring?" she asked.

"Are you kidding me? He's one of the great punk rock artists of the 80s!" said Bobby.

"Oh please, he uses the same chord progressions as The Sex Pistols. People just like him because he makes that god-awful face and stamps his feet," she said, her dark red lipstick parting to reveal a smile that nearly melted Bobby.

They spent the better part of two hours talking about music, art, and work. Ana explained that she was in-between jobs. She recently spent time decorating the interior of a few famous painters, so she could afford to spend some time in-between projects. In a place where things usually seemed to move at a rapid pace, time slowed down that night for Bobby. It felt like hours, but when Ana finally got up and shrugged on her jacket, it was only a quarter past midnight.

“Would you, umm, like to come back to my place? Just for another drink, or to talk . . .or you know, just to hang out?” Bobby stammered.

“Hmm.” Ana put her fist under her chin, pretending to think long and hard. “Well, I did have six other boyfriends I had to see, but I guess I can cancel on a few of them,” she said with a wink.

They settled back into the swing of things at Bobby's place. His apartment was on the nicer side. Hey, it pays to be a little nerdy, he thought to himself. Over a few more drinks, he learned Ana was originally from Louisiana, but decided to leave a verbally abusive mother and physically abusive father as soon as she turned 18. She sold her own works of art for a while before she realized she could make a lot more money picking out bland pieces of artwork for rich California socialites. Bobby was attracted to her need to touch him, whether it was a hand on his chest, an ankle propped up on his knee, or even the little flick of the tongue when she whispered a suggestion in his ear.

Per that suggestion, they ended the night in his bedroom. His suspicions were confirmed when Ana became the dominant one in the bed, often digging her nails into his skin and pulling him closer. The alcohol gave everything a hazy feeling. Bobby felt like he was floating, and the only thing keeping him tethered to earth was the feeling of her nails digging into his shoulder blades. They made love for what seemed like forever, until they both lay with sheets tangled about like great serpents, and slowly drifted off to sleep.

If last night had been what Bobby imagined Heaven was like, the morning after was what an all-inclusive stay in Hell would be like.

The first thing he noticed after the sunlight provided a rude awakening was a pounding headache. He was no stranger to alcohol, and he'd had some brutal hangovers, but this felt like someone stuck a hot railroad spike through the middle of his forehead. To be honest, he had trouble keeping his eyes open. The sunlight seemed to rattle around in his skull, so he covered his brow with one arm and rolled over. His bed was empty.

Just like hangovers, Bobby had experienced his fair share of one-night stands, but that didn't mean his heart didn't hurt as much as his head when he realized that his little trip to heaven only lasted about 12 hours.

He was about to go back to bed with hopes of sleeping off his headache when he heard the toilet flush. Shortly after, Ana appeared in the doorway. She had one of his Black Flag shirts on, and she looked even more beautiful with her naked lips and messy hair.

"Thought I left, huh?" she asked.

Bobby nodded.

She sat on the bed and brushed her hair. "Honey, you don't look so hot. Can't handle your alcohol?" she teased.

"I don't know what it is, but I feel like I got dragged through the gutter," he said, straining to sit up. Even his joints felt weak, like he had just worked out for a couple hours and didn't bother eating anything.

"Well, are you sure I can't do anything? I gotta run somewhere, but I can stay if you like, whip up some soup or something. It's the least I can do for letting me share the bed last night," she said, smiling.

"No, that's okay. I'm sure it's just the alcohol coming back to bite me. I'll be fine once we hop in the shower."

"Well," she said, leaning over and squeezing his thigh. "As much as I wish I could join you, I really need to get going. These snooty socialites in the Hills hate to be kept waiting."

She got up to leave, and Bobby grabbed her hand. "Well hey, I really enjoyed last night, and I'm hoping we could, you know, see each other again."

Ana took his hand in hers and gently kissed the back of it. "Well, you know where to find me, my prince," she said with a wink before closing the bedroom door behind her.

Bobby spent the rest of the day in bed. A shower didn't seem to do much for the body aches, and a bowl of soup only left him feeling queasy. He figured a little cold was a small price to pay for the great night he'd just had. He did, however, discover some pretty deep scratches after peeling off his shirt. He knew things had gotten a little rough, but these markings dug deep into his chest, and they throbbed whenever he ran his fingers over them.

The sting even felt worse when he realized that he hadn't even gotten Ana's number. He was never much of a texting guy, but all he could think about was hearing her voice on the other end of the phone.

He spent the weekend sleeping and dreaming about Ana. In those dreams, she was wearing a black dress with a slit in the side. He was tied to a chair, but he knew he was in no danger. She stood across from him in a dimly lit room, almost like those interrogation scenes in the cop movies. He heard the click, click, click of her heels on the ground as she stepped closer towards him. She whispered something in his ear, but he couldn't quite make it out as she traced a finger along his jawline and gave him a wink.

Sadly, this was where the dream ended the last two nights. Just as Ana's lips would tickle his ear, he'd wake up. The rude awakening would be paired with the realization that he was covered in sweat and the marks on his chest were inflamed and throbbing again.

He sure felt sick that week, and when he got to work, many of his coworkers noticed. His cubicle-mate Michael peeked over his monitor.

"Rough weekend, Robert? I knew you were a party animal, but you look like hell," he said with a sarcastic grin. Michael was one of those California transports from the East Coast that felt like he had to embrace the yuppie lifestyle. He had a picture of his boat as his screensaver and spent most of the time talking about the latest accomplishments of his two kids. He used every chance that he could to tease Bobby about his boring lifestyle. In Michael's perspective, he assumed Bobby used his free time to study code and read sci-fi books, and that was just fine. If he knew that he actually spent his weekends with combat boots and a leather jacket, his tormenting would almost certainly ramp up.

Bobby looked up from his monitor. "Oh, no," he said. "I guess I caught a cold over the weekend. Maybe working on this new coding project gave me a virus." He let his dry joke hang in the hair like a limp flag.

"HA! You've got a weird sense of humor, Robert, that's what I like about you. I know everyone around here thinks you're a wet noodle, but I know there's a guy full of personality in there. How's the coding coming for that refactor site? I figured you would have slept in the office over the weekend to get that shit done. If that stuffs not finished by the end of next week, the boss might get rid of the whole team."

"Well, it's certainly a task, but I think we'll hit the deadline." Bobby and his team were closing in on their biggest project to date. One of the largest online sales sites had code that was crumbling by the day. Just like the foundation of a house, the coding on a website can become too old and unstable to hold up the rest of the site. Bobby and his team were essentially tasked with building an entirely new foundation, then transferring all of the content from the old site onto the new platform. To say that was a tough task would be an understatement. Literally racing against a website that could crash at any minute, the development team was working night and day to get the project finished within the next two weeks. Although Bobby reassured Michael, there certainly wasn't much confidence backing up his words.

The work week seemed to crawl by as Bobby eagerly looked forward to Friday. While his nose was in a computer screen the whole time, his head traveled back to Ana. He could still feel her lips on the back of his hand, the way those lips parted when she flashed a smile, and the way she tilted her head all the way back when she let out a laugh. He figured the best shot of meeting up with Ana again would be to go to the place that they met the first time.

Luck would be in his favor as he spotted Ana sipping her drink and nodding her head along to the band on stage. She noticed him as he approached and immediately came over to give him a hug.

“Well hey there, handsome, I was hoping I'd find you here tonight!”

“I was just thinking the same thing,” Bobby said. “I realized I never got your number last week, so I figured this was the best place to look.”

“Well, it seems like you're in luck. I don't really use phones much, so I have no number to give out.”

“Oh wow, very 1960s of you,” said Bobby.

“Ahh, yes yes, I also arrived here in my carriage as well.”

The night continued much like the last time they got together. They enjoyed the music, talked about life in the quiet confines of the speakeasy, and both had their fair share of drinks. As they were about to leave and head back to Bobby's once again, they heard a commotion right outside the building. A crowd had gathered around a man shouting. No stranger to weird men shouting (it was L.A., after all), Bobby and Ana tried to get around the crowd and head towards his car.

"Somebody help me! That lady, she did something to me. She gave me some kind of disease," the man yelled.

Bobby stopped and looked closer at what was going on. The man clearly had something wrong with him. He had tear snot running down his face. Strands of mucus were tangled in his beard, and he seemed to be gasping for his next breath. It took Bobby a second, but he quickly realized the man was the same one that he'd seen with Ana a few weeks ago.

"Hey, don't you know that guy?"

"I doubt it. It's probably just some homeless person looking for attention. They always hang outside this place around closing time so they can talk drunk people into coughing up some change." She pulled on his arm and tried to lead him away from the crowd.

As Bobby turned away from the spectacle, the man lunged towards them both. "It was you! You bitch! What did you do to me?" Bobby and Ana both flinched as he hobbled towards them. Luckily, the man's feet got tangled and he hit the ground hard. Bobby could even hear the *whoosh* of his breath being knocked out of him. Bobby fingered the switchblade in his pocket. He'd never had to use it for anything, but he learned pretty quickly that most people in the punk community carried a knife on them, just in case things got a little too rowdy.

"It was you . . .you . . .did something to me," the man gasped as his eyes locked on Ana.

The crowd was now watching this scene unfold between the three of them. Bobby was looking back and forth between Ana and the sick man.

"Look what she fucking did to me, dude!" The crowd backed up as the man lifted up his shirt to reveal a patchwork of deep cuts that criss crossed his chest. Some were recently reopened and dark blood dripped onto the front of his pants.

"Look, dude, I don't know what you're talking about, but I think you got a bad batch of whatever drug you're on. Can we please go now?" It was the first time Bobby heard that tone in her voice. He was so used to her warm, free-flowing voice, but now she sounded cold and panicked. They walked away as the man sat up on his knees and began to sob.

"What a loony," Ana muttered when they finally started driving back to Bobby's place.

"Yeah . . .he was probably on something. You did know that guy though, didn't you?" Bobby asked, giving her a sideways glance.

"Unless we met in a mental institution in a former life, there's no way I know that nut job."

Bobby was sure that he'd seen that man with Ana before, but he didn't think it was his place to pry. He also didn't want to ruin the evening. The crazy guy with the flu almost blew his chance at another night of great company and even greater sex.

They finally got into his apartment, and Bobby shrugged off his boots and relaxed on the couch.

"I'm gonna go freshen up," said Ana with a wink. "Do you have anything to eat? I don't think I've eaten since lunchtime, and I'm starving."

"I think there's some cheese in there if you want to cut some up!" he called after her. "And bring the wine that's in there, too!"

"Oh boy, you're pulling out all the stops tonight," she called back from the hallway.

Bobby blushed and wiped his sweaty palms on his jeans. Last time they were together, he was definitely more intoxicated and therefore didn't need to overthink everything. This time, though, his thoughts and his heart were both racing. He kept thinking of the things they'd do that night, but those thoughts were getting muddled with pictures of that man crying in the middle of the crowd, snot tangled in his beard and tears leaking from the corners of his eyes.

Luckily, Ana reappeared wearing nothing but her red heels. She carried a plate of cheese in one hand and the bottle of wine in the others. She paused for a few moments to let Bobby enjoy the view.

"Now I'm a happy gal. I've got some wine, cheese, and I slipped into something comfortable."

"I think you might have slipped out of it," said Bobby.

"I suppose you're right," she said with a laugh. "I couldn't find any wine glasses, so I suppose we'll just have to share."

"I don't mind that at all."

They shared swigs of the wine, and Ana let him softly slide pieces of cheese into her mouth. She laid her bare legs across his lap, and Bobby had trouble keeping his eyes in contact with hers.

"I'm really glad we ran into each other tonight," said Ana. "I feel like we had some . . .business to finish."

"Is that so? I seemed to remember us both finishing pretty easily."

She smiled. "Oh honey, you haven't seen anything yet. I can get quite controlling sometimes, and tonight I'm feeling extra dominant."

Bobby was intrigued. He was never too adventurous in the bedroom, but with a woman like this, he was game for whatever she'd like to try. She took another swig of wine and Bobby watched as some of it dribbled off her chin, down her chest, and disappeared between her breasts.

The alcohol was starting to hit him just as she led the way back to his bedroom. Everything seemed to flash by in short, blurry clips. One second he was following Ana through the doorway, the next second he was lying across the bed and watching as Ana slipped off her heels. He felt the dull burn of her hand on his chest and the flittering of her tongue making its way down his neck. His entire body felt numb, and he barely felt her teeth dig into the flesh between his neck and collarbone.

The room grew darker and for a while, all he could hear was the sound of his own heartbeat. The steady thump quickly accelerated when he saw shadows begin to swim across the room. Ten foot figures danced across the ceiling. Dark creatures with horns watched above as if they were medical students observing a procedure.

He gasped as a shooting pain ripped through his chest. He looked down and saw the handle of his own switchblade sticking out of his chest. Behind it was the crown of Ana's head, and she began lapping up his blood. She looked up for a second and Bobby let out a moan.

"What's wrong, sweetheart? I told you I was hungry! I'll be finished in a few minutes, and then you can get some rest."

Bobby's last image before he passed out was Ana licking the knife clean and leaning her head back before letting out a laugh.

ABOUT THE AUTHORS

James Pyne

James Pyne was born in New Glasgow, Nova Scotia. He has appeared in *The Pulp Book of Phobias, Clockwork Wonderland, Creatures in Canada, a*nd many other anthologies in the last few years. His debut novel, *Big Cranky: Fall Into Darkness*, will be re-released soon, along with the rest of the trilogy. Subscribe to his email list at https://www.mothmanpublishing.com/ for important updates and free short stories, novel excerpts, and promotions.

Michael S. Collins

Not yet dead or undead, Michael S. Collins has been writing horror since childhood (blame RL Stine!), and was formerly a Fortean Times book reviewer. He is currently an editor at Other Side Books. Other recent publications include Sea Terrors, co-written with Jon Arnold and Jo Thomas. Michael lives in Glasgow with a family, but has no pet vampires...yet.

Luke Frostick

Luke is a British writer based in Istanbul. He writes the books column at Duvar English and is the editor of the Bosphorus Review of Books.

B.J. Thrower

B. J. Thrower is experiencing a career resurgence, selling ten short fiction stories in the past two years. "Parasites, a Tale of Route 66," in *Todd Sullivan Presents The Vampire Connoisseur,* is her second, recently published horror story. She has upcoming publications of two dark fantasy flash fic pieces in Eerie River Publishing's *Dark Magic Drabble Collection* anthology (2021), and a s&s novelette in Weirdbook #49. She's previously published in Asimov's, the old pro sf magazines Aboriginal SF and Artemis, in the 2019 horror anthology, *Guilty Pleasures and Other Dark Delights* by thingsinthewell.com, and in many others. She's a professional SFWA member, and the 2020 Vice-President of OSFW (Oklahoma Science Fiction Writers). Find her on Facebook at **B.J. Thrower**, where she blogs about the writing life under the heading, "Looking for Nessie." Her website is at: http://bjthrower.osfw.online. She lives in a bedroom community of Tulsa, OK, with her husband, the mysterious "R".

Gary Robbe

Gary Robbe is an educator and writer currently living in Colorado. His fiction is generally dark regardless of the genre, and he has had numerous stories published in e-zines, magazines and anthologies. Gary is a member of the Horror Writers Association, Denver Horror Collective, and Rocky Mountain Fiction Writers. He is also an associate editor for Bewildering Stories Magazine. At the moment he is working on a novel that should be ready in the next few decades.

Keawe Melina Patrick

Keawe Melina Patrick is a fiction writer with a fondness for the dark side. Being a geologist with an addiction to writing leads to horror, suspense, and all things murderous, because geologists aren't afraid to get dirty. Other passions include archery, her huskies, Koa and Kai, and hiking the Big Island.

Tony Pisculli

Tony Pisculli is a Hawaii-based writer whose work has appeared in The Arcanist, Daily Science Fiction and Grievous Angel. He blogs about writing (and swords) at LoveBloodRhetoric.com.

Paul Alex Gray

Paul Alex Gray writes linear and interactive fiction starring sentient black holes, wayward sea monsters, curious AIs and more. His work has been published in Nature Futures, Andromeda Spaceways, PodCastle and others. Paul grew up by the beaches of Australia, then traveled the world and now lives in Canada. On his adventures, Paul has been a startup founder, game designer and mentor to technology entrepreneurs. Chat with him on Twitter **@paulalexgray** or visit www.paulalexgray.com

Gordon Linzner

Gordon Linzner is founder and former editor of *Space and Time Magazine*, and author of three published novels and dozens of short stories appearing in *Fantasy & Science Fiction*, *Twilight Zone*, *Sherlock Holmes Mystery Magazine*, and numerous other magazines and anthologies. He is also a copy editor, a licensed New York City tour guide, a sound technician, and lead singer for the Saboteur Tiger Blues band, among other odd jobs. He is a member of HWA and a lifetime member of SFWA.

Nicholas Stella

Nicholas can often be seen scribbling away on scraps of paper at the oddest of hours and in the most random of locations, as inspiration has no respect for time or place.

Max Carrey

Max Carrey currently lives in sunny California, but will be moving to a gloomier location much like the settings in her stories (hopefully without the tragedy and mayhem involved). She has many tales already in print, but has forthcoming horror in GLAHW's Marisa's Recurring Nightmares, Pavor Press' Sonorous Silence, Red Cape Publishing's F is for Fear, Weasel Press' Incendiary, and more! To stay up to date follow her at: instagram.com/maxcarrey/

Priscilla Bettis

Priscilla Bettis read her first grownup novel, The Exorcist, when she was a little kid. She sneaked the book from her parents' den. The Exorcist scared Priscilla silly, and she was hooked on the power of the written word from that moment on. Priscilla has been an engineering physicist and a swim team coach, both wonderful professions, but what she really wants to do is write . . . or die trying, probably at the hands of a vampiric wraith. Priscilla shares a home in Virginia with her two-legged and four-legged family members. Find Priscilla online at priscillabettisauthor.com.

Lisa Hario

Lisa Hario grew up in the Midwest, a voracious reader and comic book geek with a soft spot for vampires. She currently resides with her partner, He Who Toils Endlessly, in a house run by the wee dictator. Her website is darkisnotevil.com.

Troy Diffenderfer

Troy Diffenderfer is from Lancaster, PA. In October of 2018, Troy released his debut short-story collection "White Noise" with Owl Publishing. The collection generated buzz due to its unique concept. Diffenderfer took rock n' roll songs spanning four decades and turned these songs into horror stories. In 2019 Diffenderfer partnered with a local artist to publish a coffee table book titled "Killers: Portraits of the Depraved." This book featured 33 drawings of serial killers, each with an accompanying piece of flash fiction that delved into the mind of each killer. In his spare time, Troy enjoys spending time with his wife, Lydia and his dog, Bowie.

Jacob Floyd

Jacob Floyd lives in Louisville, KY with his wife Jenny, his two dogs (Tarzan and Pegasus) and three cats (Baloo, Narnia, Pandy, and Baby Bat). He and Jenny have written five books about the paranormal, one about aliens, and one about strange and unusual mysteries. Jacob has written three horror books. Together he and Jenny are known as the Frightening Floyds.

ALSO AVAILABLE FROM NIGHTMARE PRESS

THE UNTAKEN
By Bekki Pate

They're in her room again. She watches them glide silently closer. She closes her eyes against the threat of their presence. Long, bony hands roam her body. It's happening again, and again there's nothing she can do about it. There's a bright flash of light, and they take her.

Charlie Samuels is an abductee. She's used to that now, never knowing anything different, and she's almost in control of most parts of her life. But a new threat appears, something made from nightmares, something designed to target people like her.

Charlie soon finds herself wrapped up in a conspiracy much bigger than she ever imagined, and the beings she has spent her entire life running away from may have been on her side all along.

THE CURSED DIARY OF
A BROOKLYN DOG WALKER

by Michael Reyes

There's something strange going on in Brooklyn. Occult chants ring out in the dead of night from quaint brownstones and trendy coffee shops. The stench of blood-soaked orgies and human sacrifice wafts through yoga studios and food co-ops. The servants of the demon star have come to power. And they are hunting for the only soul that can destroy them.

RETRO HORROR

Twelve tales of old-school drive-in-style horror

WHOOPS! I WOKE THE DEAD
by Joseph Rubas

A teenage girl with an ancient spellbook accidentally wakes the dead on Halloween night.

VAMPIRE SERIES OF EXTREME HORROR BOOK TWO:
THE GRAY MAN OF SMOKE AND SHADOWS
by Todd Sullivan

A rogue vampire seeks revenge on her abusive uncle while another vampire hunts her.

VAMPIRE SERIES OF EXTREME HORROR BOOK ONE:
BUTCHERS
by Todd Sullivan

Vampires hunting vampires in the no-holds-barred bloodfest set in Korea.

ANIMAL UPRISING!

A lion, a hybrid, a bear – oh no! A goat, a gull, and a big black dog! Can't forget the roaches, the deer flies, and the tarantula hawk, or the abominable insect that rises from the earth! We got creepy crawlers and killer critters for everyone. Oh, you want mythical creatures? How about a malevolent spirit posed as a fox, a rambunctious jackalope, or a herd of unicorn-gazelles on a distant planet? Let's not forget the supernatural silver stag with the power to raise the dead. Oh, did I mention the giant mantis shrimp? Yeah – we got a giant mantis shrimp. Humankind really has their work cut out for them in this collection of terrifying tales of beastly butchery. Need to know more? Check out *Animal Uprising!* for all of the mayhem.

CHAINSAW SISTERS
by Jacob Floyd

An amnesiac woman believes her dead sister is talking to her through a chainsaw, asking her to seek revenge against the men who killed her.

NIGHT OF THE POSSUMS
by Jacob Floyd

JACOB FLOYD

Man becomes roadkill as mutant opossums rise up and attack a small Kentucky town.

Thank you for reading! If you like the book, please leave a review on Amazon and Goodreads. Reviews help authors and publishers spread the word.

To keep up with more Nightmare Press news, join the Anubis Press Dynasty on Facebook.

Printed in Great Britain
by Amazon

54625711R00144